To Aleane & you

FINDING HOPE

A COMING-OF-AGE HISTORICAL ADVENTURE

LYNN BOIRE

A little 'Canadiana'
to honor our parents.

Enjoy!

Lynn

Cover design by Steven Novak

ISBN eBook: 978-1-7771458-9-7
ISBN Print: 978-1-7771458-8-0

DEDICATION

Dedicated to Angie,

my kind, loving, and supportive sister.

CHAPTER 1

August 1937
Big River, Saskatchewan

J im gritted his teeth as mixed feelings of regret and excitement coursed through his veins. This experience of following in his pa's footsteps was what he wanted, wasn't it? To be treated like a man and share the load his father carried? Nevertheless, he couldn't help but feel anxious as he stared at the black and white wooden coach beside the tiny school in his hometown. It held so many happy memories of his friends that he was leaving behind. Every October since he started school, the Madsen family would cart the coach to their farm, the furthest away from the school. The old pot-bellied stove inside would be cleaned, the wheels exchanged to iron sleds and checked for wear, the harnesses oiled and repaired. By then, the windy, icy days of the Saskatchewan winter would not be far away.

Jim could almost hear the teasing laughter of his friends, Brian and Stephen, the lilting music of the harmonica that

Lucy played. This year, his friends would pass the Madsen homestead without stopping for him. This year, his seventeenth, he would begin to shoulder the load of a man beside his father. He would not finish his schooling. There were more practical life skills to be learned, and Jim was eager to discover them.

There was no use in wishing things were different. Jim sighed as he accepted the need to set aside his childish ways and his childhood friends. He couldn't be with his friends and discover his pa's world at the same time. Jim was tall and strong for his age, and his father needed him. No longer would he spend the winters separated from him, boarding at the Madsen's for the school year. Now Jim would pull his weight and learn the fur trade. He'd help set and monitor the trap lines with his pa along the myriad lakes and rivers north of the winding Churchill River. He couldn't wait to go there, to see what drew his pa to the north country for months at a time, year after year. His breath quickened in nervous anticipation.

"Jimmy!" A hoarse voice called out to him, interrupting his thoughts.

"Coming, Pa," he returned. Time to quit daydreaming and prove himself.

Dennis Taylor heaved another fifty-pound bag of flour over his shoulder and steadied himself before packing it into the neighbor's old truck. "There's plenty more to haul, son. Get the lead out."

"Yes, sir." Jim knew that this supply his father had brought up from Big River would be their last. Within the week, they had to be prepared to head north and start to lay aside their other winter supplies. Two hundred pounds of flour, a hundred pounds of salt, a pail of sugar, two buckets of lard, tea, beans, barley, and tobacco would be carefully divided into the three freighter canoes. Each canoe would also have the necessary oil skins, a long pole, axes, knives, guns, and ammunition, as well as an extra set of winter clothes, all tightly bundled to conserve every inch of space. Jim looked at the staple supplies and swallowed hard. It didn't look too good as far as he was concerned.

"Is that it, Pa?"

"Yup... it's all we can pack. Ya'll be cursing even this much when we start to portage. We'll get the rest of the food we need once we arrive at the camp." His father leaned against the truck and mopped his forehead, his face grey and pasty. Frowning, he looked up, saw Jim's worried look, and confronted the youngster.

"Yer sure you want to do this? I'm not a cripple yet. I can handle the route myself, y'know."

"I know, Pa," Jim replied.

"We'll be living on fish 'n game," he warned. "This isn't a picnic."

"I can handle it. I'm not a kid anymore," Jim replied quickly, trying to hide his anxiety, but the high pitch in his voice belied his uncertainty.

"Right you are. Let's move it," Jim's father commanded. As Jim sat in the truck, his father went inside the mission, returned with a small package bound in oilskin, and threw it in with the rest of the supplies. It was almost nightfall before they returned to their run-down home on the edge of the Madsen's farm.

DENNIS FELT the fatigue tugging at the edge of his mind and knew he had made the right decision to bring his son along. As he was gone an average of five months out of the year trapping, Dennis never felt the need to have a fancy place for the brief time they lived together in the spring and summer. As far as he was concerned, a summer job on the farm, a roof over their heads, and bunks to sleep in were all they needed.

As the overloaded truck approached their home, the dogs began to bay. Their keen sense of hearing knew the sound of their master's vehicle, and they waited impatiently for him. The relationship between Dennis and his dogs was intensely close and loyal. It had to be, for they each depended on one another for survival. They stood tethered outside the two-room cabin, eagerly awaiting their freedom and the owner's attention. Dennis had learned long ago to leash them. Otherwise, he would soon find they had followed him wherever he went.

Against the side of the cabin leaned a pair of twenty-three-foot freighter canoes, a combination of birch bark, canvas, and spruce root lashings. Because Jim would be accompanying his father, they added an older sixteen-foot canoe for extra supplies. Yesterday, Jim had helped his father seal the seams and lashes with rosin, then applied another coat of linseed oil to the rest of the canoe to keep the materials waterproof yet supple. Oiled dog harnesses hung on hooks, curing in the waning sunlight.

Their preparations were nearly complete. Jim helped his father unload the truck, which would then be returned to the Madsen's. Just as in summers gone by, Jim cooked for his father often. His pa was happy to hand over the chore of meal preparation after a winter of trapping. After the first disastrous summer of cooking, Jim returned to the big house, eager to learn how to find and gather natural herbs and spices to flavor the basic dishes his father ate. Mrs. Madsen also taught him not to overwork the dough and make a decent bannock that wouldn't be heavy or hard on the teeth.

Jim hoped his father remembered to bring pepper. He was eager to accompany his father but wasn't old school. He didn't feel he had to go without all the necessities, and as a young man, he enjoyed his food too much to settle for bland food. Surely, a pound of pepper would not jeopardize the trip. He also secretly stuffed the farmer's almanac and a deck of cards among his clothing. It was hard to imagine what they would do after a day's work. And once he was up there, he knew it could be months before they would come in contact with another person.

Jim went indoors to fix their supper, putting some salt pork on to cook in milk before frying it with onions and potatoes. He set the table and put the bread and honey on the side for dessert. When he ate with his father, he noted the sharp contrasts between them and the family he had boarded with for the past six years since his mother's death. Food had one purpose for fur trappers like Dennis, and that was to sustain life. Consequently, variety and taste were not of utmost importance like in the Madsen home. Jim heard his father attend to the dogs with fresh water and kibble, talking and roughhousing with them. He finished making a pot of tea and then called his dad for dinner.

"Nothing fancy for dinner."

"Don't need anything fancy. I've been keeping ya so busy ya haven't had time for hunting. Maybe we'll hit the blinds at dusk and see if we can't land a few ducks to keep us going." His pa took a small portion from the iron skillet, then sat to eat his supper, tipping his mug to Jim to fill it with tea.

"I'd like that. I'll roast the birds tomorrow." Jim filled both their mugs with strong tea and joined his pa. After watching his pa push his food around his plate, hardly eating anything, he added, "Maybe you'll have a better appetite for the duck."

"Don't have much appetite for anything these days. Don't worry about it." His pa pushed his plate away and reached for the bread and honey before switching the subject. "Mrs. Madsen's baking apple pies today, and she'll send one over tomorrow. She says she's going to miss us. Nice family. They've been real good neighbors. The place is still ours when we get back if we want it."

"Why wouldn't we want it? This is our home, right? We'll be back by late spring and be helping them again on the farm." Jim was surprised at his pa's comments. "We're not moving, are we, pa?"

"No, no. This is home once the trapping season's finished. Do you remember what I told you 'bout tomorrow?"

"Yessir. Recheck the knives. Check the guns over and make sure they're oiled and ready, then wrap them in oilskin."

"Right."

"What are you going to do, Pa?"

"I have to arrange to have all our stuff hauled to Beauval. I always leave on the seventh of August, that's less than a week away. That way, by the time we hit the Hamilton River, it should be low enough to handle the rapids. It's a helluva lot easier to pole the river than portage."

"That's good, Pa?"

"Unless ya like packing the loads more often than ya have to. Then we'll head to Ile-a-la-Croix. We'll stay a few days before paddling northeast on Clearwater Lake to the mouth of the watershed. Our cabin's at the tip of the second inlet on the left. People know it now as Taylor Arm. That's our home base." Dennis pulled away from the table and took a package of smokes from his pocket. He grabbed his matches and lit his smoke, but after the first inhale, the coughing started again, causing his eyes to water. Angrily he stubbed out the cigarette, missing the comfort it once gave him.

Dennis watched his son clean the kitchen and prepare for a sunset hunt. Dennis drained the rest of the tea to stop the aggravating tickle in his throat and thought of his friends who tried to stop him from returning to the Churchill River Basin from another year of trapping. *There's no place I'd rather be to breathe my last breath on this earth.*

Addicted as Dennis was to the wide-open spaces of the north, there was only frustration this summer for those who tried to talk him into seeking medical help and retiring. He was as stubborn as an old bull moose. As the August nights grew slightly cooler, Dennis could feel the deep yearning growing inside him. The lure of the silent, desolate marsh-lands beckoned him irresistibly. The beauty of deep blue lakes with white beaches stunned him every autumn. Dennis felt nature's friendship and reveled in it, even as the frigid winds began to blow, turning the colorful wilderness into a stark winter land of white.

Then the rivalry began. Dennis hoped Jim remembered his warning about nature, the whore. She'd give ya many things and promise to provide for ya, but unless ya worked wisely and treated her fairly, she'd betray ya and let ya die.

"Understand me?" his pa had asked.

"Yessir. No sir, not really," Jim said.

"In the autumn, nature's beautiful, warm and bountiful.

If yer not careful and only see what's there in front of ya, yer in danger of losing her favors. Ya have to nurse what she has, set aside goods for the winter, and never take her for granted. If ya don't prepare for the future, she'll take great pleasure in watching an ignorant man suffer."

Dennis shook his forefinger slowly at his son to catch his attention. "Same's true for the animals and fish we catch and hunt. Some men trap muskrat and mink and whatever else they can find, wherever they find it."

"What's wrong with that? We're trappers. That's what we're supposed to do."

Dennis shook his head slowly. "Think about that." Dennis tapped his temple emphatically. "If ya take every-thing ya can get yer hands on, what happens? Sooner or later, there's nothing left to trap. Yer only hurting yerself. Ya have to leave the animals in the creeks alone—only take from the rivers and ponds. Otherwise, before ya know it, there's nothing left. The animals from the creeks renew the rest of the area, just like the creek's waters fill the ponds and the rivers. A trapper should only take where there are lots of sign. Otherwise, the northern wilderness will end up the same as the south when they trapped everything in sight. It's almost barren of furs now."

Dennis breathed a sigh of relief as he saw his son widen his eyes. He was glad Jim took his explanations seriously. God willing, he'd be there to guide his son back home, but Jim had so much to learn if he had to return on his own. But the kid was smart. He'd train him like the Denes and Crees taught him. He'd be fine.

It was probably time to share more details of his trap-ping life, so he tapped his mug for a refill of tea. He crossed his feet stretched in front of him and motioned for Jim to sit beside him.

Jim's excitement grew as he listened to the details of the route. How thrilling to have an area named after your pa! Ever since he found out he would be accompanying his father this year, he began packing a fifty-pound sack of grain for an hour, resting, then hiking again across the fields and low hills surrounding the farm. At first, he barely made the hour without stopping at least three or four times. His muscles ached, but his determination to pull his weight on the trip grew. He felt more confident now that he could haul for three or four hours with only a few rests and still have some energy left.

In the evenings, he practiced rifle shots at a makeshift range under his father's tutelage. He had so much to learn, and he enjoyed it all. His only worries were when he saw his father, gripped in paroxysms of coughing, collapse weakly. This summer, Dennis hacked more than ever, and his color wasn't good. Jim wondered if he'd be capable of surviving the trip if something happened to his pa. As a tendril of fear snaked down his spine, he pushed the thought aside and joined his pa on a walk to the slough south of their home. Jim slowed his pace so his pa could keep up with him and kept the conversation as lively as possible. Hopefully, his chatter would be enough for him to avoid talking.

AT FORTY-EIGHT, Dennis looked back on his life with little remorse. He lived life as he chose, a solitary figure content to face the north wind. He enjoyed living in the wild, pitting his skills against the odds to earn a living. In earlier days, the money was no better than what you could make farming. Now, with the depression hitting the country, he came out ahead. It wasn't the money. However, that was important to him. It was the peace and solitude he ached for, the pride he felt whenever he came home to the interconnected waterways of the Churchill River Basin and his familiar traplines.

There were many things he still had to teach Jim before his time was up. He couldn't wait much longer. He hated admitting it, but his strength had waned in the past two years. The persistent cough could drain his energies to a point where he was forced to neglect his lines until he regained his strength – a terrible situation that Dennis could no longer justify handling the responsibility alone. If he couldn't harvest the traps, it would be a waste of animal life, and he couldn't, in clear conscience, abandon his catch to the grey wolves or wolverines. He only hoped he had enough time to introduce his skills to Jim, gradually introducing him to courage and inner strength. These qualities would ensure a proper introduction to manhood. He could go to his grave secure that his son would create his success, independent of others. Trapping honed your senses, made you self-reliant, a beggar to no one. Not a bad legacy to pass on, he decided.

APPEARING CONFIDENT, Dennis vigorously shook hands with Brother Wilfred. "*Merci, encore.* I'll see you again in the spring, *si Le bon Dieu veut.*"

"*Au'voir, que Le Dieu te'garde.*" Brother Wilfred replied. He blessed Dennis and Jim with the sign of the cross, offering a prayer for a safe and successful winter. As a spiritual presence for his small parish, Father Wilfred and the missionaries spoke a language containing a smattering of indigenous phrases as well as English and French.

"Goodbye, Jim." Brother Wilfred reached out and shook his hand as he watched Dennis walk towards the canoes with his dogs. He motioned Jim to approach.

"When you return, perhaps you can talk your father into staying with us. With the new Central Farm Program, the government is allotting ninety-nine-year leases of forty-acre plots. You could apply and have your own home and farm to work instead of returning to Big River."

"But that's home for us, and it's where I've grown up. I don't think pa's up to starting all over again."

"Mais, ton Pere needs to slow down, make life a little easier for himself. You'd have friends here to help you. There will be many opportunities when the immigrants arrive to farm the area. You'll do well here. Promise me you'll talk to him this winter. I'm so glad you'll be with him this year. I've worried about him out on his traplines alone."

"I'll do the best I can and talk to him, but I doubt it'll do any good. He's set in his ways. Good-bye, sir. And thank you for your help." Jim replied politely.

"C'est rien" he replied. "Mais ecoute," Father Wilfred checked to make sure they weren't overheard. "Tu devrais prend bien soin de ton Pere - he's a sick man." The oblate squeezed Jim's shoulder and raised his voice. "Listen to your pa. He's a wise man. We'll be watching for you in the spring."

Jim nodded and reassured him he would try his best. To keep up with his French-speaking friends outside of school, he had picked up some slang phrases and could piece together most conversations. Jim gave him a two-fingered salute as he walked away.

His eyes scanned the familiar countryside again. His heart tightened as he thought of his friends now, still at home during the summer break and working the fields most likely. He had tried to see them all before leaving to say goodbye. The only one he missed was Lucy, who had been taken to the hospital in Prince Albert for appendicitis. It hurt to go without seeing her again. He hoped she'd recover soon. He was the only boy she'd ever kissed, and he knew without a doubt that they were meant for each other. It didn't matter that her parents disapproved of him. She did, and his young heart drooped at the thought of leaving her. He dreamt of her last night, her lilting French accent whispering her love for him.

"Jim!"

"Yessir!" Jim tossed his dream aside and helped his father put the canoes in the water, tying them to the nearest tree so they could load their supplies. The water was warm as he waded knee-high to the skiffs, carefully packing the supplies so that the weight would be evenly distributed and not top-heavy. His father guided him, advising which provisions should go down first to reduce the chance of losses in case of a tip-over. Within a few hours, they had completed their task.

"Are ya hungry, son?" Dennis asked.

"Not yet, Pa."

"Good. You take Chimo, Bear, and Lucky with you. They're older and steadier. I'll take the two other dogs." Dennis chuckled as he watched Jim slap at the sand flies attacking him. "Ya better get used to that, son. I've seen days where those devils come in clouds."

"Don't they ever bite you, pa?" Jim asked.

"Can't get through my tough hide," he laughed. He choked a little, the laughter turning into a coughing spasm. Dennis turned aside while Jim walked away to the lake shore, looking for a pocket of clay. He mixed a dab on his palm and smeared it on his neck like his father had shown him. He heard his father gradually getting control of the ravaging cough and returned, offering a cup of water.

"Thanks." Dennis sipped at it gingerly, testing the acceptance of the cool refreshing liquid to his parched throat. His eyes were red-rimmed, his face still flushed with exertion. "OK. Let's go."

Jim called the dogs, and after taking a last look around, he untied the ropes and scrambled into his canoe. The dogs swam to the boat and, with hardly any help from Jim, clambered in, shook themselves off, and settled down to bask in the sun. Jim lifted the paddle and guided it effortlessly through the calm, warm, velvet waters, following the ripples of his father's canoes.

Slip over, stroke, glide, stroke... Slip over, stroke, glide. The rhythmic, silent paddling hypnotized Jim. They paddled north, more or less following in the middle of the wide Hamilton River. Jim scoured the landscape and called out to his pa whenever he saw a white-tailed deer or an otter hiding as still as a statue in rushes along the shore. Now and then, in a burst of energy, he would paddle furiously to overtake him, enjoying the thrill of his new adventure. Around 5:00, a light breeze blew up, gently bristling the leaves of the cottonwoods. Jim looked at his father with pride. No wonder he lost him to this each year: how could he begin to compete with this beauty?

As they approached an incoming stream, his father stilled his canoe and pointed his paddle to either side. "Put yer dip net into those pools. I'll pull my canoe up, and we'll break for some dinner."

"Are we camping here tonight?" Jim asked hopefully.

Dennis knew that his son's muscles must be aching. He

had paddled recklessly in the afternoon, from sheer pleasure, he was sure. He would have to learn to pace himself. "No. We should be able to put in another two or three hours after dinner. We won't settle for the night until around ten o'clock. It's dusk here until almost midnight in August."

Dennis navigated to shore and started a fire. He watched his son row close to the calm holes and lowered his net into the shallow waters. Dennis swiped his hand over his mouth, hiding a grin as he watched Jim scooping the waters, often coming up empty. He'd soon learn the difference between the shadows and the importance of timing. The fire was crackling, glowing embers heating the rocks surrounding the pit when Jim brought the canoe and his catch ashore.

"That was a lot harder than it looked. I had to keep moving the canoe back into the right spot." Jim said.

"Ya'll get the hang of it. Not a bad haul for yer first time." Dennis remarked as he saw the catch. He watched his son cut up the whitefish and throw it to the dogs.

Jim gut the walleye, throwing the guts to the dogs, and brought the filets to the fireside. He grabbed the old cast iron skillet and, after melting a pat of lard in it, browned the walleye, then hooked it over the fire. Bannock was already cooking on a hot rock close to the glowing embers.

Jim went to the stream and filled a pail of water. He stretched his legs and arms, twisting his shoulders from side to side to release the tiny knot. The smell of the smoky fire, the frying bannock, and sizzling fish drew him back like a magnet. He sat down, relaxing and watching his father.

"Don't you ever get lonely, Pa? I mean— it's beautiful here, but it's so big... so quiet."

Dennis shrugged, then grinned as if he was about to share a secret. "The first few days a man comes out are the worst. After that, ya love the silence and enjoy the peace.

Except listen, hear that?" A family of mallard ducks called to each other as the rippling waters of the lake whispered at the shoreline. "It's never really quiet. There's life all around us, and it's rather noisy right now. Wait until the cold arrives and the first snowfall. Then ya'll hear what quiet's really like."

From the look on Jim's face, Dennis realized just how important this trip was. The boy hung on every word he said. To be fair, he'd never really talked to him like this before. His wife had always been the one the boy turned to, and by the time she died, Dennis had no idea how to handle entertaining a young boy. Seeding was in full gear by the time he returned from the traplines, and the long days of a farmer's life left little energy to figure it out. Dennis never had time for idle chatter with anyone, and as the years passed, their relationship was a caring but impersonal one. He'd broken the ice a few times as he explained their journey, but he wanted a better relationship.

Now it was time to change that. After the simple meal and tea, Dennis told his son to clean up. As Jim reloaded the gear, his father carefully put out the fire and checked his directions and the time. The water had calmed again with the daily change in wind direction completed. They continued paddling northward, each silently enjoying the pallet of colors the evening sky created as the sun began its descent. Jim followed his father to shore, hauling the canoe onto the beach as much as possible, tying the bow to a branch. He gathered some wood and started a fire in a rocked-in circle. Obviously, this was a regular stopping point.

"Is this your place, Pa? Do you always stop here?" Jim asked.

"Yes. This one I usually use if it's been windy or I'm

behind schedule like today. I have my special stopovers. Look closely over in the bush, and ya'll see a lean-to. I have them regular-like along my traplines too. Over the years, I've built small line cabins every thirty or forty miles with basic tinned goods and a heat source. If the weather's bad, I can always spend a few days there and wait it out. Over the years, people like me have prepared for the worst. That's why we're still around."

Dennis returned to his canoe to retrieve his oil skin and gun. "Well, what are ya waiting for? Grab yer stuff, lie down by the fire, and don't forget the mosquito bar unless ya want to get eaten alive."

"Pesky critters, aren't they, Pa?" Jim asked as he slapped his pant leg. He felt like the insects had invaded every part of him. He could hear them buzzing around his ears, and the backs of his hands were already bitten. The smudge from the fire was helping some, but Jim's exhaustion made him overly annoyed at the constant attacks from the mosquitos.

"Throw some more leaves on the fire, and the smoke drives them away. If the wind picks up, ya'll find a difference. Meanwhile, fix yer bed. The nights are short. We'll hit the first rapids tomorrow."

Dennis called the dogs to return from their explorations. They lay at his feet, fully content to be near him. He watched Jim remove a few sharp rocks underneath him before settling down and calling Chimo and Lucky over to lie by him. The crackling fire was slowly dying, the ruby embers throwing a warm blanket of heat.

Dennis looked up at the sky, admiring the clear night that held thousands of sparkling diamonds in her cloak. He felt tiny and insignificant in the grand scheme of life. He heard his son snoring softly and took his cue. Tomorrow would be a long day, and the real initiation would start when they met the rapids. He hoped his son would be up to the challenge. It would be his first test, and his attitude would be his first proof of whether Dennis was right in bringing him here or not. He shivered in anticipation. With luck, they should reach Buffalo Narrows and the village of Ile-a-la-Croix within the next four or five days.

JIM STRUGGLED with the bag of flour across his shoulders. He was near the end of emptying his canoe, and the last items were the heaviest. He stumbled over the trampled trail, his boot catching on a root. Damn, he thought, but he didn't say a word. No way did Jim want his pa to think he couldn't handle it. The sweat was trickling down his forehead and temples as he determinedly put one foot ahead of the other, willing the distance to shrink.

It was their third portage in two days on the Hamilton River. The curvy river ran from west to east. Then at times, it would veer from south to north. His father explained the differences they would have encountered had they left earlier. The water level was at a good point - low enough to see the dangerous rocks and use their long pole to maneuver around them, yet high enough that the rapids could not damage the heavily laden canoes. It was a more dangerous route, yet the time and energy it saved them made it worthwhile.

There were drawbacks, of course - one had to portage cataracts. Now Jim understood the careful attention to weight and necessity. The warm August days sapped his strength as he carried the loads from his canoe to the next good stretch of river about a half-mile away. Scrambling down the inclines with a load on his shoulders consumed all his concentration. He kept his eyes glued to the trail before him, avoiding any hazards. One more pack to go, then he would help his father unload his. It saddened him to see his once robust father, wheezing and coughing, struggling valiantly to keep up.

The buzz of sand flies, now a continuous accompaniment, no longer bothered him. A branch swung and caught him in the cheek, but that didn't slow him down either. Nor could the aching muscles in his forearms and shoulders. He needed to prove himself, and as he lowered the sack onto a log, he took a short rest, waiting for his pa to catch up.

"Why don't you rest for a while, Pa? We could stop for lunch. I'm starving." Jim hoped his pa would stop and eat if he felt that Jim needed it. It probably galled him to realize he couldn't keep up with his muscular seventeen-year-old son, so he needed to tread carefully to avoid injuring his pride.

"Yeah. I'll get some grub for us. Can you manage the rest?"

"Sure, Pa." Jim climbed through the brush again, retracing his steps. It must be galling for his father to leave the heavier items for his son to carry. Jim had grown up watching his father work twelve to fourteen hours a day, his muscular frame seeming never to need a rest. He hoped it wasn't too obvious that their positions had reversed.

Wiping the sweat on his sleeve, he paused briefly to splash water over his head and drink several handfuls before returning with another load. Thank God they only had two more to go around before entering Clearwater Lake. Jim knew this section was only the training ground compared to the Churchill River Basin. Although cataracts in this pre-Cambrian shield area were not high—often a drop of no more than thirty feet, they posed serious problems.

His pa had warned him they'd have different problems once they left the lake and entered the marshlands. It was a much slower-moving river, marbled with deep, calm pools edged by marshes and sloppy mud bars. Moving northeast as they were, the streams would empty into narrow, shallow lakes, then drop twenty feet or more where they'd connect to another shallow lake. This pattern continued across northern Saskatchewan and Manitoba to finally empty into Hudson's Bay. With the load they carried at this time of year, the last leg would be extremely tough. Hopefully, they could get through with more poling and fewer portages around the falls.

Jim looked at his pocket watch. 11:00 a.m. Not quite noon, but his stomach was growling. They were up and paddling after morning light, so the tea and bannock were long gone. Jim hoped his father would have some meat for lunch. As if in answer to his thought, he heard a shot ring out, and he smiled. He figured he had another three loads to transport, then by that time, whatever his pa shot should be cooked.

He whistled a tune as he approached the canoes, observing the land around him. They had recently passed through a section of land that burned out three years ago from a lightning strike. The charred Black Spruce dotted the landscape in eerie forms. Yet life was already showing signs of returning. Red Saskatoon berries and wild blueberry bushes had miraculously taken hold, and near the river bed, Dennis had shown Jim the tracks of bears coming to feed. Jim stopped and picked a few handfuls of berries, the tartness making his tastebuds sour. His father also pointed out the tender young shoots of birchwood and jackpine taking root. Jim surveyed the landscape and marveled at nature's ability to heal itself. He hoped the summer had been lenient around their cabin on Taylor Arm.

An hour and a half later, Jim washed up quickly before sitting for lunch. Dennis had shot a fat partridge, and it was roasting over a small fire. The three older dogs were resting after a meal of fish netted by Dennis, while the younger two were investigating the area and chasing each other. Jim noticed how seldom his pa seemed to speak now. The further north they traveled, the more reticent his father became, and likewise, so did he.

"Dig in, son - go ahead." Dennis encouraged.

"Smells good—I'm starving." Jim helped himself to bannock, partridge, and some tea, then gobbled it hungrily to appease his appetite. Dennis watched him and smiled inside, remembering how ravenous he used to be when younger. He seemed to have lost his appetite lately.

"Have another piece of bird."

"No, go ahead, Pa. I got enough."

"I don't need as much as a young man. Go ahead – eat."

Jim grabbed another leg and bit into the crispy, dark meat. So far, he had enjoyed the rabbit, duck, and partridge over the rangy beaver. The fresh fish they usually had for dinner was his favorite, although anything was good when Jim was hungry. He looked forward to getting settled and shooting a deer or a moose to augment their menu and was anxious to try caribou and bear. This land was full of new sights and experiences, and Jim was eager to be a part of it.

The hot tea relaxed him, and he joined his Pa in a short rest. An hour later, full and refreshed, they traveled onwards, navigating the waterways and marshes. Jim followed his pa's lead and kept a sharp eye on the areas where he pointed. Thank God he had a great memory. He had a feeling he'd appreciate it later.

"Ya saw that otter skittering through those reeds, did ya? Ya got a sharp eye, son. Before ya know it, ya'll be as fast as yer ol' man."

"Thanks, Pa. I'm catching onto the signs I ought to look out for like you told me."

"Good to see where they are now before the ice and snow gets here. That's where we'll set the traps for mink and otter. Concentratin' on yer surroundings is important, son. It'll save yer life one day."

As Jim became more adept at spotting and shooting a rabbit or partridge as easily as his father, he reveled in his pa's nod of approval or his occasional words of praise. Jim's eyesight was lightning quick, and after learning to recognize the signs, Jim could often predict where they would likely see mink, otter, and deer.

Skillfully netting a cache of fish under his pa's watchful eye relieved Jim. The long winter required a supply of several hundred fish to be caught and dried. The fish served as food for the men and the dogs and bait for the traps. Dennis estimated they would settle at their cabin and be ready to harvest the first run of spawning fish by the first week of October.

While sitting near the campfire one evening, enjoying the growing quiet as nature prepared to sleep, Dennis took another opportunity to open up. He looked at his muscular son and felt proud that he could also consider them friends. He knew he'd made the right decision to bring him on this journey.

"Did I ever tell ya of the fall I was delayed - the year your mother died?"

"No, sir. Ma died August the 8th, didn't she?"

"Yes. 1933. By the time the funeral was over and I found a place for ya to live, I was behind three weeks. To tell the truth, I didn't have the energy to hustle as I should have. I missed the bulk of the whitefish season and could only set aside around three hundred fish. I wasn't too worried, though. I figured I'd drop a couple extra caribou when the migration came through and smoke it."

"Caribou's good meat, isn't it, Pa?"

"Not bad when yer hungry. Not as good as deer or a good fat moose, though. It's too lean, not enough fat, and tastes mighty gamey. We need fat for the winter in our diet, but if that's all we got, it's better than nothing. Anyways, that year as luck would have it, the Caribou didn't pass our way. The ice came as usual around the beginning of November, and usually, the barren ground Caribou start their southerly migration a few weeks later. The dogs always knew when they were near. They'd race through the bush, always going north, if I'd let them. They'd go off their feed and wouldn't touch the fish I gave them. Not that year."

Jim sat quietly, listening to the tale that Dennis wove. He watched him roll and light another cigarette, then prodded him to continue.

"What did you do?"

"Nothing much I could do. I set my traplines, watching for signs of their coming. I was lucky enough to shoot a couple of bucks, and as time wore on, I put the dogs and me on rations. A few hundred miles northeast of our cabin, there had been a large fire I hadn't heard about. The caribou skirted it and passed our area rather than go their usual route."

"Well, you made it," Jim replied.

"Yeah. I made it. I lost twenty pounds and one dog, but we survived. The dogs and I hadn't the energy to go very far on the lines, which meant our take was much smaller that year." Dennis paused to catch his breath and leaned against a log to close his eyes. He heard Jim go to the river, refill their mugs, then touch a cup to his hand without a word. Dennis gripped the cup, set it down, then rubbed his chest in a circular motion. He knew if he could slow his breathing, he'd eventually regain his strength.

Twenty minutes later, as he felt the color return to his cheeks, Dennis opened his eyes and sipped his water, then carried on the conversation as if nothing had happened. "When the spring migration brought the white tail back, we gorged ourselves for two days. I'll never forget it. I felt like a new man."

Jim logged that conversation in his mind. He didn't have the experience to chance missing the fish run. He'd make sure they'd arrive by the first week of October - no matter how hard he had to work. Jim refused to let his worry show as he smiled. "I guess so. Maybe we should call it quits early today, pa. Start fresh in the morning. What do you say?"

"Nah. We'll take an hour, though, then start repacking the canoes. We'll see how we feel after that. Are ya getting tired, son? Might not be a bad idea to start fresh in the morning with loaded canoes."

"That sounds good to me. We've put in long hours each day, so we must be ahead of schedule. It wouldn't hurt, that's for sure."

Two hours later, they re-loaded their canoe, then returned to the campfire to relax. Jim netted some whitefish which his pa gutted and shared with the dogs, before slapping the remainder in the hot skillet. Picking a handful of wild blueberries, Jim folded them into the bannock dough and then fried it in another pan, bringing new interest to their taste buds. The conversation was sparse as they each used the time to recharge their energy for the following day.

Every time Jim thought things would get easier, he'd get a surprise. He wondered what was in store next. Whatever happened, he was now confident he could handle it. Panic and worry were not words in his pa's vocabulary, and they wouldn't be in his either.

CHAPTER 2

After an encounter at the last portage with a black bear, the men were fortunate to only sustain a two-day setback in their timetable. They'd been lucky that the bear was long in the tooth and not as aggressive as young bears. It had happened so quickly that all Jim could remember was the fear freezing him in his tracks when the bear rustled from the brush onto the river bank. Less than forty feet were between them when the smelly, fly-infested animal turned his nose up and sniffed his presence.

The harsh yell from his pa triggered his reaction to shoot it. Jim's headshot had hit the mark, followed by another one by his father. The bear flopped onto its side. Fearful of other predators coming to check out the noise and the smell, they quickly hung it, skinned it, then gutted the animal before quartering it.

Jim retrieved the salt pail, liberally sprinkled the hinds, then wrapped it in an oil cloth. Dennis noticed his son frequently looking over his shoulder into the brush.

"Jimmy, finish what yer doing and load the canoes. Best to leave before the wolves catch the scent and come looking for the guts." Dennis turned aside, covering his mouth to hide the smile from the visible relief that came over his son. He needed to remember how new this was for him, and it would take time for Jimmy's nerves to settle. They paddled for a few hours before Dennis angled towards shore to another of his lean-to resting places. That night, neither had any energy left for a fire and chose to shake out their bedroll under the shelter and collapse.

Two days later, they were once again reliving the experience.

"It's amazing, Pa. It almost feels like we've had a holiday. The food and the rest were just what we needed. I'm not used to this life yet." Jim was sprawled on his bedroll beside the fire with Chimo snuggled up against his calves. "You're looking better too. You were starting to worry me. Most mornings, I had to nudge you a few times to get you up."

"I'm not the man I used to be, that's for sure. I've been pushing hard to get to home base, but this is a good time to take a break. We'll finish smoking the bear meat and leave in the morning. We're only about two days away from Taylor Arm, but it's tough territory, going through the marshland. It changes some from year to year, and it's always tricky to sidestep the bogs. I'll take the lead, and we'll use our long poles often to make sure we keep floating through the channels. Once we clear that, it's maybe four hours paddling to reach our home base."

Keeping track of the days, Dennis was pleased to see that despite their delay, they had reached his cabin on October 4, 1938. The first three days they spent unloading and re-organizing the cabin. Dennis cured the first batch of snares and traps in cauldrons of boiling water, laced with birch bark and wood ashes, before instructing Jim to take over. It seemed there was a never-ending list of jobs that Dennis needed to teach his son.

Jim proved quick to learn, and his natural dexterity was invaluable, often taking over tasks as he saw his pa's energy falter. Mending fish nets, erecting the racks that would dry and smoke fish and game for use during the winter, or chopping wood to stockpile in the lean-to behind the cabin, there was never a dull moment until after the evening meal. Then Jim and his pa would take their tea outdoors, discuss the day's results, and enjoy the tranquil, deepening twilight.

JIM TOOK a break from chopping wood and splashed water over his face and head. Even though the days were cooling, the physical exertion and continuous pace of preparation took their toll. He scanned the property, catching sight of his father with a gun hitched under his arm, heading into the bush with the dogs. His pa would return with fresh game and a smile after contributing to their food stores. At least Jim could spare him the reality of his declining health by taking over the more arduous tasks.

He was learning so much, yet he still felt like a rookie. After eating some fried rabbit, fiddlehead ferns, bannock, and tea, Jim leaned back and patted his stomach. "You're not a bad cook, Pa. I'm surprised."

"What do ya think? I've learned to forage from the Crees. Until frost, I gather Chaga mushrooms, fiddleheads, and plantains to eat fresh. Some years, I've even dried some for the winter. Whenever I can, I'll harvest wild rice over near the marshlands and store that too."

"Did you see the honeycomb I brought in yesterday? The idea to smudge them worked great. I got buzzed, but I never got stung. I wrapped it in oilcloth, but you'll have to show me what to do next."

"Told ya. We'll tackle that in the morning. I have several empty tins on the top shelf, just waiting to get filled. I've even been able to dry berries on the odd year that there's a late Indian summer. It's a real treat to have something sweet during the dead of winter."

"I can imagine. It's amazing how much stuff I see now. Keeping my eyes open and noticing everything around us has surprised me. Now I never miss a chance to gather supplies for the winter."

"True. Then again, ya never had to fend for yourself. The Madsens were always there. By the way, I think it's time to start building yer toboggan, son. Let's make it our next job to finish. Tomorrow, I want ya to paddle upriver and find yerself a young birch tree. After you limb it, tie it to the canoe and bring it back. We'll need to de-bark it, and then I'll show ya how to peel it lengthwise to make the skids." Dennis saw his son's eyes sparkling at the challenge.

"Sure!" Jim's excitement began to show as his knee bounced with anticipation.

"Ya better bring two back in case we have a problem. Lots of work to do to curl the ends. We'll need to boil water and steep the front of the wood. Then we can curve them the way we want."

"I'll grab the axe and some rope and go now. There are still a few hours before night settles in. I'll bring my gun and maybe pick up some dinner for tomorrow night too."

"No rush, wait until morning. It may take ya longer than you think." Dennis smiled, then patted his son's shoulder a few times before standing up and turning towards the cabin. "I think I hear my bed calling me. G'night, son."

~

DENNIS THRUST the blade of his shovel into the edge of a hole now measuring almost four feet wide when he heard his dogs greeting Jim's canoe. He leaned on his shovel, and as he shaded his eyes to watch his son's approach, Dennis noticed a covey of grouse peeking from the front of his son's canoe. Two birch logs hooked to the stern bobbed along behind. Grinning, he walked to the shoreline, caught the rope Jim tossed to him, and pulled steadily until the canoe was embedded in the gritty sand.

"Ya did good there. A couple of twenty-footers ought to give us lots to practice with. Might even get a second backup toboggan out of them. Ya don't want to have a busted-up sled in the middle of winter. Damn near impossible to make a new one then." Dennis took a few of the birds Jim handed him and eyed them. "Nice. Roast bird tonight."

"Sounds good. I was thinking the same thing, Pa."

"True. It's damn near impossible to make a new one then." Dennis helped him haul the logs onto shore, then returned to the cabin for the dog harnesses. "Might as well have the dogs help you whenever possible. They're used to pulling weight. We'll drag them closer to the firepit and start peeling them."

They finished digging the hole to a three-foot depth the following day, then lined it with clay from the shoreline, letting it harden in the warm sunlight. Then Jim built two separate fires and filled two large cauldrons with water to boil. Watching his pa skin a birch then peel a ten-foot strip two inches thick was impressive. With guidance, Jim pealed another ten-foot strip and brought it to the homemade tub.

The men stopped for a long lunch while waiting for the water to boil, and Dennis explained the next step. "When the water's steaming hot, pour it into the clay tub. Then fill the cauldrons again to boil, so we have more hot water when we need it. We'll dunk the ends of each strip into the bottom of the tub and let it soften. Ya have to keep adding the steaming water until the wood's workable."

Dennis retrieved his toboggan to show his son the curves they wanted to achieve. "Yer aiming to have a two-foot section of softened wood that we can wrap part way around one of those stumps you see by the shed. We'll tie it around the stump as quickly and tightly as we can. Then it has the curve we need for the sled when it cools. Sometimes, ya need to dunk it several times until you get the right amount of curve. Understand?"

"Doesn't sound like it's too tough to do. Then after it's cooled, we start building the rest of it?"

Dennis grinned and slapped his son's back. "Let's see what ya think when yer finished. It's not as easy as it sounds. After the curve is set, we'll start sanding and oiling the skids to run smoothly on the snow before making the platform. It won't be finished in a week, son. Probably more like two weeks before ya have your sled—and that's if ya don't split the skids."

They worked well together, the apprentice noting each step to prepare for winter. Both the cabin and the smoke-house were organized with the necessary wood chopped and piled. Now it was time to stockpile supplies for the winter.

They hunted for rabbit, geese, and partridge, slicing most of them into strips and smoking them into jerky to travel the traplines. When Jim shot his first buck, he glanced at his pa as he proudly approached his kill.

"Clean shot, son. Right through the shoulder. I'd say he's dead but never take it for granted."

"If he's not moving, he's dead, isn't he? How can I tell for sure?" Jim continued through the brush towards the back of his kill, then stopped abruptly when his pa yelled at him.

"Stop right there." Dennis caught up with Jim, pulling him back from the deer's legs, making a wide berth. "Those hoofs are like knives. If he's only injured and stunned, he could slit ya—right through yer pants, slash yer skin and even sever a muscle." He took a knife from his belt and cautiously approached the deer's head. Dennis placed the blade against the open eye, then glanced at his son.

"If he's still alive, he'll blink. If he's dead, he won't move at all. Then yer safe to gut him."

"Anything else I should know?" Jim grumbled. He wondered if he'd ever absorb all this knowledge.

"Remember when we shot the bear and had to hurry like hell to get out of there? I told ya a gunshot in the wild is like a dinner bell. Wolves and bears are either used to the sound or get nosy. And if they get a whiff of the gut bag, they'll be coming to get it, and yer gonna be in trouble. Keep yer gun handy. They'll fight ya for the deer if they're close by. So be quick and do yer gut, then drag the kill from the area as soon as ya can. They'll be content with the guts for a while."

"All I can remember is that I was scared out of my mind. I forgot about the dinner bell. Thanks, Pa." Jim took a rope from his backpack, made a twenty-foot double pull line, then wrapped a double knot around the deer's head. By this time, his father had gutted the deer and was ready to head home.

"Let's move." They both grabbed a rope and began the trip home. Dennis kept an eye around them, occasionally stopping to catch his breath and listen for anything following them. Under protest, Jim took his pa's rope and wound it around his chest and over his shoulder for the rest of the way. When they returned to base two hours later, Dennis instructed his son to hang the deer high up a tree about a hundred feet from the cabin. They'd let it hang a day or two, then begin the smoking process.

When Jim returned, he washed up and entered the cabin, half expecting some food to be ready. They'd been gone for most of the day, and he was starving. Instead, his pa was laid across his bed, deep asleep. Thank God Jim had eased his load by hauling both ropes. Jim removed his boots, covered him with a blanket, then stoked the wood stove. He left the house to get some smoked rabbit from the winter cache, then returned to mix dough for bannock. Left-over beans from yesterday would round off the meal and fill his hunger.

He thought the smell of food would rouse his father, but it didn't. Jim worried about whether to wake his father or not. He lit a kerosene lamp to eat his dinner by, and soon his exhaustion and full stomach convinced him that it wasn't unusual for a man his pa's age to need more rest than him. He pushed aside the fear of what his pa's ailing health would bring. Now was not the time to worry about that. What will be, will be.

Waiting for the fish run was more nerve-wracking than Jim thought it would be, probably because he didn't know what to expect. Each day his pa would paddle out to the main creek feeding the lake and check the count. Then they'd work on last year's nets while Jim checked his loops and knots against the expert. There was always wood to cut, game to smoke, and traps and snares to maintain and learn to use.

Finally, the run arrived, heralded by the sound of hawks announcing their appearance. They dip netted their fish for a week, hauled them to shore, and gutted them before going to camp and drying them. Placed high on racks, the salted slabs were covered by old netting and dried over a slow smokey fire. Dennis showed his son how to cure it, then pack and store it in the underground winter cache. By the end of the third day, Jim was doing most of the work, giving his pa time to rest and explain everything they had to have ready before the freeze-up.

The beauty of fall only reminded them further of how close winter was. The willow, birch, and tamarack ablaze in autumn glory bent gracefully in the wind. Their leaves fluttering and dropping warned them of the coming season. There was a sense of urgency in their preparations for winter.

No time was wasted.

Dennis whittled a branch tip and drew a map for Jim in the sand near the beach. He placed a cross near the water's edge. "This is our camp." He dragged the tip several feet before making a "Y" in the sand. "Our traplines run north to northeast, covering almost a thousand square miles."

"Holy smokes, Pa. That's a lot of territories to cover," Jim's mouth fell open as he ran his hand through his hair. "How the heck do you cover it all?"

Dennis ignored the question and drew the main traplines and subsequent branches until he reached the brush. "Grab some rocks and put'em where I tell ya." Dennis returned to the shoreline and indicated the positions Jim should drop them. "The rocks are the larger ponds in the marshlands. The lines are the rivers and streams we set our traps on." Dennis returned to the branch and began making crosses on various traplines before drawing a line across the top third.

Jim sat on a piece of driftwood and eyed the map, swallowing a lump in his throat. *How the hell was he going to remember that*? It looked so much larger and more complex than the paper map his pa had given him. A frown creased his forehead as he watched his pa grin at him and light a smoke. Suppressing a cough, his pa shrugged and tossed it aside.

"Don't worry, son. The dogs know the routes like the back of their hand. They'll always bring ya home or to the closest shelter. See the crosses?" Dennis pointed to each of them. Most were smaller, but a few were quite large.

"Yes. Are they your camps?"

"They sure are. As soon as the first ice forms, we'll start making trips to each of them and make sure they've got tinned supplies. We'll cut kindling and some wood at each one. It'll be easier to warm up the place if the weather forces us to stay a few days."

"How many lines have you got?" Jim's slow and deep voice betrayed his apprehension.

"We have thirty lines ranging from fifteen to forty miles. They run parallel, just like the creeks that drain the marshlands. Most of the lines connect at one place or another." Jim pointed to the line he drew across the map."I only use the areas above here at certain times of the season when chances of snowstorms are low, and I know the yield will be high." Dennis paused to catch his breath, ignoring his son's worried stare.

"Below the line are the ones we regularly set and harvest. I trap one section at a time for a few weeks before moving on to the next one. It works."

Jim stood and walked around the map, trying to memorize the pattern. He looked up and saw his pa studying him. Jim sucked in a breath and pulled his shoulders back. "It looks simple enough."

"Good man. It is." Dennis pointed to the dogs wandering near the cabin. "Ya can depend on your dogs. They know where to go because they've been doing it since they were pups. And they can sense changes in the coming weather or predators nearby that ya might not see at first. Trust them. Use yer common sense, and ya can't go wrong."

Jim nodded and accompanied his pa to the shed, where he pointed out the traps and gear they'd use to stock the shelters along the lines. The men hadn't long to wait after processing their fish before the icy north winds began to blow, inviting the waters to freeze. As soon as the ice was thick enough to walk on safely, Dennis led Jim across the narrows and set the closest traps, explaining each step. Watching his son find a good spot and safely set snares created a bond between them of trust and confidence.

When the marshlands froze, they took their toboggans out, followed the creeks and rivers, and cleverly stationed their gear to catch the curious fox, mink, and otters. Every day, they expanded their route, leaving dried goods at the line cabins for future use. As the ice on the lake became thicker, they made their ice hole which they would keep clear all winter, for fresh water and fish.

Jim loved it. The overpowering stench of fish spawning in the river beds was gone as the ice formed. The cold air was still bearable, and he enjoyed the fresh crispness. He wished he had a beard like his father. Right now, his whiskers were few and far between. He kept his parka tied tightly and was comfortable in his new role as a trapper. His pa taught him the basics he needed to maneuver his toboggan, running behind it and pushing a loaded sled up the inclines, helping the dogs with their work. But essentially, it was up to the dogs to do—and as they were well experienced, Jim counted his blessings. Excitement and a joyous feeling of freedom overcame him when occasionally he would jump on an empty sled for a ride, and they would fly down the ice. He'd never known its' equal.

"See this?" Dennis rested his team and motioned to a river that emptied into a narrow part of Taylor Arm. "Pretty frozen, hey?"

"Yup."

"This is the first ice to freeze. When the caribou come, this is where the herd cross. In early winter, it's safe, good ice. But in mid-winter, watch out. Once we get some snow, it protects the ice. But sometimes, a strong current from the river beneath works away at the ice and melts it, so there are often open holes." Dennis pointed to the creeks emptying into the lake. "When traveling down the lake, sometimes ya can see the vapors rising, and ya know a creek or river's nearby. Sometimes ya don't see the hole - the ice hasn't quite melted, and the snow's almost floating over it. If ya don't know what to watch out for, yer' gonna land the whole shebang in the lake."

"No thanks - I think I'll stay far enough away from the shore. A mistake like that could kill me." Jim replied.

"True. The bitch of it is, that's where yer going to get the best yield of mink and otter. Yer bound to get a good setting wherever there's moving water."

Jim groaned. "Makes sense. Nothing comes easy, right Pa?"

"Ya got that right," Dennis agreed.

As the weeks went by, it wasn't hard to believe this tranquil, glacial setting could devour a hapless trapper. Jim looked around, appreciating the contrasts he saw. The deep blue sky was cloudless, and against it, the icy branches of the bushes and trees perched starkly white. He often wondered with awe at how sneaky nature was. A cursory glance would suggest there was nothing but death and stillness here. Yet the land was teeming with activity for those who knew where to look. Already they had twenty-two foxes, six otters, and two minks to prepare. He breathed in deeply, enjoying the chilly air, exhaling a misty vapor. He felt strong and alive as never before.

After extending the lines along the lake shoreline, enough snow had fallen so they could venture inwards and set the other lines. Winters in central northern Saskatchewan were frigid and clear. Often the snow amounted to not more than twelve to eighteen inches in depth.

The first time Jim let the dogs have the run, he was frightened. They tore down the trails at such speed that sometimes the toboggan would skid and bounce off a tree. He noticed the missing bark from the occasional approaching tree and realized how old some of these trails were. Since they were pups, Dennis had trained the dogs on them, and they knew the route by heart. It wasn't hard to believe Pa when he retold stories of coming home in the dark on his team's instinct alone. On the return trip heading south, the dogs intuitively knew they would get a few days' rest and be well fed. Their enthusiasm to get home was catchy, so Dennis often let them run.

While the dogs received their due and rested, Jim helped his pa with the skins. They did the freshest first while the frozen ones were left until last. They would tie those together and lower them into a hole in the ice where they would thaw naturally.

Jim marveled at his pa's dexterity. After carefully cutting the fur around the paws and eyes, he hung the carcass from a strong branch. Dennis opened the carcass at the anus and cut part way down each hind leg. After a quick brushing to remove matted fur or debris, his pa meticulously separated the pelt from the membrane of the body. Next, he'd peel the hide down, bringing fur against fur until the whole skin was off the body and inside out. His pa would insert a shaped board onto which the hide would be stretched and tacked down. Then, he'd strip it of any remaining fat. The pelts would dry for several days before they were bundled and stored away. Although Dennis did his work with a knife, he only allowed Jim to use a sharpened stone, the Indian way. It was slower to do but safer as an inexperienced stroke could cost a pelt to lose its value. Worse yet, the trapper could lose a finger.

As months passed, Jim often experienced the loneliness he thought he would. He could now go on traplines by himself, taking charge of the runs closer to the cabin and looking after the skins. His father took the longer lines and was sometimes gone for a week to ten days. Dennis traveled past the burnt-out, unproductive areas into the maze of shallow lakes, marshes, and rivers. That area's narrow strips of water attracted a natural wildlife crossing, resulting in excellent trap yields. Long forages up there were well worth the effort.

Jim grew accustomed to the silent, busy life. The first few long journeys his pa had embarked upon had filled Jim with uncertainty. He was thankful for the smuggled deck of cards to keep his mind occupied. The last couple of days were spent with an eye on the lake, watching for an approaching speck to be his father. Now he was used to seeing the odd caribou lying on the ice resting and had stopped wondering which speck was which. With this experience, Jim knew that his Pa would return - even if he were delayed.

They had only seen one person in four months - a Dene

nicknamed Beads. He stayed with them for a few days, chewing the fat, and traded a pair of snowshoes to Jim for a box of ammunition. He accompanied Jim on a few runs and gave him new advice, showing him when he missed obvious signs of activity.

Only once had he been allowed to join his pa on the longest forty-mile route and camp outdoors. It was thrilling to hear for himself the snap of the trees as they cracked with frost and know that he, too, had beaten the odds. Jim was amazed at his father's ability to camp beside a fire consistently in one of the seasonal lean-to structures, although sometimes it was only the night sky above him. At temperatures that could sink to 20 and 30 degrees below freezing, he was glad the Denes had taught him how to survive in such weather.

That was the first trip he witnessed a massive display of the Aurora Borealis, the eerie dancing lights of the northern sky. Its shimmering, lime green waves played against the mauve twilight, then disappeared as suddenly and mysteriously as they came, leaving both Jim and Dennis awestruck. "It never gets old," his pa had remarked. Jim could see the truth to that.

"Hı, Pa. Good to see you. You have a nice load there," he greeted his father. Jim hid his concern about the trip and busied himself untying the dogs and feeding them. He grabbed the heaviest packs and was relieved to see his pa pick through for the lightest load. Jim glanced over his shoulder often, watching his pa slowly return to the curing shed with small armfuls of furs.

"I had a good setting - there's three silver lynx in there. That ought to be worth a couple of ten spot each for sure."

"Holy mackerel," Jim whispered as his eyes shone with pride. Lynx were prized furs, with a limit of seven per year in that area. Jim hauled in some pelts already prepared, obviously beside an evening fire. The more animals he could skin, the longer he could travel and check the snares. However, the shorter nights took away precious time for fur preparation, so the bulk of Dennis' cargo was still carcasses.

When the weather had turned blustery and howled for four days straight, Jim worried more than usual about becoming a trapper like his pa. The tree trunks bent to unbelievable angles while branches ripped from their core. Jim stayed close to the cabin after being caught on the second day in a blizzard that was frightening in its intensity. The cold seared his nostrils, made his sinuses ache, and his eyes burn. He had found refuge among the jackpines and huddled with Chimo until it passed. For him, solitude and dangerous weather might not be worth the beauty and independence his father craved.

Each day afterward, Jim paced the cabin floor, concerned for his pa's safety even though Jim knew he'd probably survived even worse. He played solitaire with the now well-worn cards until he couldn't stand their sight. Reading the almanac for the second time was preferable to another losing game of patience. Frustrated, the first tendrils of anger began snaking through his mind. *What the hell was he doing here?* Why, oh why had his father brought him to this isolated place?

Yes, there was beauty here. *Yes*, Jim had learned a lot of things he would never have in Big River. But what good would that knowledge be if his pa never returned? Jim struggled to keep his spirits up as time passed at a snail's pace.

Hiking in his snow shoes every afternoon, Jim looked for signs of approaching movement. Finally, three days after the storm passed, he caught the distant sound of dogs barking. Jim finished bringing another load of wood to the cabin and stoked the stove, making sure it would be toasty for his pa. Looking inside the pot of soup he had made the day before, he added a handful of barley to thicken, knowing his pa would welcome the hot meal.

His worries were well-founded. His pa's eyes were burning, shrunken lights encased in a feverish face. Determination emanated from him, and Jim knew he would not rest until the toboggan was empty and all the necessary details looked after. Between trips to the storage shed, Jim put a kettle of water on to boil inside the cabin for tea. It wouldn't take long to serve up the simple dinner already simmering. Finally, they paused.

"I have some water on for tea, and there's some leftover soup. Won't take me long to make some biscuits either."

"Thanks, son." Dennis coughed and spat aside on the snow. Jim saw the red splotch on the snow before Dennis' boot kicked snow over to cover it. Jim felt his guts sink and his heart race as he saw the evidence of his father's health.

"How have you been feeling, Pa? You don't look so good."

"Same's usual. So-so. C'mon, let's go and eat. You fed the dogs, didn't you?"

"Sure did." Jim watched his father turn and hobble to the cabin. The man had a fever. No doubt about it. What was he going to do? Why was that man so stubborn? Didn't he care? Jim gritted his teeth as he followed his pa inside.

"Well - where are we on your calendar, son? I figure that was the last storm of the winter. The days are getting warmer and a bit longer. The crows are back, and most of the caribou are gone. Must be near the end of March."

Jim walked over to the calendar and noted the crosses had almost consumed March. "You're right, Pa. It's the 28th today." Jim's raised eyebrows showed his surprise. "How do you do that?"

Dennis shrugged. "It's in the bones. Do this long enough, and yer going to feel it too. Even the dogs know the changing seasons." He knew the signs of spring well, and he was rarely out more than a week either way.

THIS PAST TRIP to his most distant traplines was Dennis' last for the year. The trails were losing their snow pack, causing mud in the marshlands and making it harder for the dogs. It was time to concentrate on the beaver hunting as the ice broke on the lake. The beavers flourished around Island Lake slightly north of Taylor Arm, and the long twilight evenings of early spring were a favorable time. The frisky mammals were often too eager to enjoy their freedom from the imprisoning ice to avoid danger, becoming easy prey.

The last storm of the winter almost did him in, but Dennis made it. He looked at his son with pride as he ate the hearty soup. He'd been right to bring him here. Jim had grown from an uncertain, awkward youth to a strong, confident, and skillful young man in one season. The tickle in his throat began again, and then all thought was driven away by the relentless throes of another coughing spasm.

Jim helped his father to his bed and propped him up against the wall with a pillow. He covered him with a blanket and stoked the fire to warm the cabin more. When the coughing spell passed, Jim took two aspirins out of their meager medicinal supplies and gave them to his pa.

Jim went outside, leaving a cup of tea with honey beside him to sip and ease his throat. He hung the carcasses and started the long job of skinning them, concentrating on the exacting job. At least this was a chore he could do well, whereas worrying about what to do with his father was useless.

When Jim let himself think of what could happen if his pa didn't survive, his jaw clenched with frustration. As much as Jim treasured his time getting to know his pa on this trip, a thread of fear tied his stomach in knots. *What was his purpose in pushing himself to the max just to die out here?* His pa was not only risking his life, but he was also risking Jim's too. *He was a greenhorn, for crying out loud!* Jim buried the anger and fear down deep inside.

Jim scraped the membrane forcefully, concentrating on using up his nervous energy. There was nothing that could be done about it now. He just hoped all the information he'd absorbed would be enough to bring him home, should he have to navigate his return trip on his own. By the time the carcasses had all been cleaned and stretched to dry, Jim wasn't surprised to return to the cabin and find his pa sleeping. His last trip proved too strenuous for him, but his pa was never one to give up.

Three days later, Dennis seemed in better spirits and was anxious to bring Jim to shoot beavers. The snow on the lake was uneven now—the sudden warming after the wind storm had slowly melted any pockets of ice that had southeastern exposure. The caribou droppings from the last migrating herd absorbed the heat much faster, and the piles sank through the three-foot layer of ice. Some of the pools in the narrows and creeks were already breaking from the fast current. Colonies of energetic beavers would be foraging for food and fixing their lodges. That would be the last type of fur they would gather before heading south.

"We don't need the furs, Pa. We have plenty. Let's organize the camp and get ready to head home." Jim couldn't help but notice how the clothes hung on his pa's slender frame. Dennis now paced himself carefully, a walking stick his constant companion. He often leaned against a tree as he caught his breath, and his footsteps were slower and more deliberate than four months ago. His pa was a stubborn man who wouldn't admit his worsening health and certainly wouldn't take kindly to Jim pointing it out. Sadness simmered through Jim as he looked for a way to protect him.

"Too soon, son. Won't take long to put this place to bed. I want another trip with you. Make an old man happy, and let's see who can bring back the most pelts." Dennis spread his hands in front of him. "I'll bet you five bucks that I'll bring back more than you by the end of the week."

Jim saw the sparkle in his pa's gray eyes and couldn't resist his challenge. His pa ought to know another trip would be dangerous for his health. But, if that's what he wanted, then Jim wasn't going to deny him that pleasure. "You're on. But you need to give me some pointers," he smiled as he shook his forefinger.

~

"KEEP FACING THE NORTH WIND, son. Make yerself invisible and watch for movement. With this weather, it won't be long until they'll come out from their dens, check out the fallen branches, and patch their homes." Dennis dropped his walking stick and leaned against a jackpine, sliding down to a sitting position. "Might as well rest when ya can, it might be a long afternoon."

Dennis knew that excuse didn't fool Jim, but his son let it slide. They had come to know each other well, and his son accepted his stubborn ways. Yielding the lead position had been a hit to his pride, but Dennis tried to take it gracefully. There really was no other choice.

"Stay here, pa. I'm going to circle the pond and get behind their den."

Hiding in the willows and brush along the shore, Jim crept stealthily towards the mammoth den that looked to cover the shoreline for at least fifty feet. He had learned that some beaver dens were over a hundred years old. The sticks and wood had long rotted away, leaving an immensely dense mud structure full of connecting passages. As twilight deepened in the still evening air, a head emerged swimming towards the opposite shore, his wake barely noticeable.

Dennis shot once, the blast reverberating. He saw Jim pop up in the brush across the pond and hollered at him. "Beat ya to it."

Surprised, Jim hadn't noticed his pa moving into position and grumbled at his lost chance. He doubted there'd be any more nosy mammals showing this evening. He stood up and made his way back to help retrieve it. "Nice one—must be fifty pounds."

"Hmm. This beaver's an old one, probably more like sixty or seventy pounds. Wasn't so hard, was it? We'll leave this place and spread out. Ya go west, and I'll go northeast. Take only one beaver at each lodge. Be patient, and yer gonna bring home a good load. I'll give ya a hint." Dennis leaned forward as if sharing a secret. "Ya can trap these fellas too, so if ya want to cover a larger area, set yer traps and return a few days later. It saves time. If there's nothing in the trap, wait for evening and shoot one. We'll keep it to day routes and compare our catches at the cabin every night. Ok?"

"Sure, Pa." Jim looked at him and hesitated, wondering if he should continue. His pa didn't like a fuss made over him. Jim took a deep breath and stared into his pa's eyes. "Are you sure you're ok to travel by yourself? I could go with you."

"I'm as good as I'm ever going to be," Dennis replied gruffly. "And by the way, boy, ya remember how we talked about people dying out here?"

Jim swallowed the knot in his throat and nodded.

"Well, if I go before the ground's soft, say a prayer and let me down the ice into the lake." If Dennis noticed the tears filling his son's eyes, he ignored them. "It's the way of the North, son. A fact of life and death. It's what trappers like us do."

Jim nodded, unable to speak yet. His pa continued, "And honestly, if I have to pick my time and place, this is where it would be," his arms encircled the area. The still night almost upon them was clear, and the air could have been considered balmy compared to the windy, frigid days of winter.

"Alright, Pa - but not this year, ok? Tough old bird like you must have a few more years left."

Dennis knew Jim was looking for reassurance that would calm his growing fears. Dennis thought his son's instincts were probably correct, but there was nothing either could do about it. "Better to keep your mind off of it, son. What will be, will be. Now, let's see who can get the most beaver pelts!"

Jim jumped at the challenge to chase his fears away. In an unexpected gesture, he went and wrapped an arm around his shoulder. "Ok, Pa, you're on. I'll make a fire here for dinner, and then we'll head home."

The men made camp on the shore, lighting a fire and skinning the beaver into a flat pelt. They took the thighs to cook for themselves and threw the rest to the dogs. Finally, with their bellies full, they carefully extinguished the fire and returned to the cabin.

JIM KNEW the territory well on Taylor Arm and scouted it, looking for the largest lodges. He planned to shoot or trap in the early morning, so he was often gone before daybreak. Evening counts alternated who caught the most, but five days later, Jim's total was almost double of his father. Altogether they had eighteen beaver pelts and fourteen weasels. It was the most time-consuming, boring trapping he'd ever done, and Jim was disappointed. On Friday evening, he approached the cabin with his carcasses and noticed the opened door on the cabin.

"Pa!" Jim hollered. There wasn't any smoke rising from their chimney, and as he came nearer, he noticed the other dogs running to greet him. "Hi boys, how are you doing?" he greeted them, rubbing their backs.

They looked excited to see him, almost frantic. Jim wondered what was making them nervous. It wasn't like them to be yipping and agitated unless—

"Pa!" Jim hollered again as he ran to the cabin. Bursting through the door, he stopped short. Laying on the bed was the shrunken, still frame of his father.

"Pa? Oh, God... Pa? Can you hear me?" Jim knelt beside the bed and put his hand on his father's fevered face, turning it towards him. His eyes flickered open, then closed again. Jim ran to get some water and gently lifted his pa's head, encouraging him to drink. The water trickled inside his parched lips and down his chin, for he was powerless to swallow in his weakened state.

Jim felt his pa's gaze on him, his eyes burning brightly. As Jim watched his father's hand moving under the blanket, he pulled it aside, trying to help. Beside his pa's thin body, empty of all the pride and energy it used to hold, was a leather-bound diary. Jim felt his chest constrict in agony, knowing the end was near. He realized his pa dared not speak, for it would certainly cause another coughing spasm that Jim was afraid he wouldn't survive. Jim's eyes filled with tears he refused to shed. "Is this what you're looking for?"

His pa nodded, reached out, and put his hand on his son's strong arm.

Dennis nodded weakly, pushing it towards him. He tapped his chest, then pointed to his son, grimacing. "Ya—ya did good, son." Dennis gasped before the coughing started again. As Jim tried to prop his Pa's head, he heard the rattling of blood in his lungs as Dennis struggled for another breath of air.

"C'mon, Pa, take it easy. I'm here now. I'll look after you. Take it easy now."

"Out-" Dennis managed to gasp. "Out-."

Dennis stared into his son's eyes, knowing full well that his son knew what he wanted. Jim gathered his frail body wrapped in blankets and took him outdoors. Underneath the clear, open sky.

His dogs bounded over with their tails wagging, happy to see their master and possibly anxious for a feeding. Dennis looked at each one of them. Instinctively, they began to whine as if sensing the impending loss and curled up at Jim's feet, trying to get as close as possible to their master.

Dennis surveyed the land around him, the bright blue sky, the barren branches of the birch and tamarack. He could smell the stand of jackpine behind the cabin, feel the warmth from his loyal teammates, and hear the crows' cawing. Spring. He was in the arms of his son.

Dennis felt the burden lift from his heart. He'd done his job well. His son was strong and independent, confident in his abilities, and he'd be ok. The strain of waiting for him to return was finally gone. Dennis glanced about again, spotting a rare whooping crane leaving his perch on a crag. His eyes blinked in appreciation of this unusual sighting. Jim followed his father's glance and saw the crane soar with his mate close behind.

Jim held him there for a long time, thinking of how close father and son had become. Jim became an adult on this journey and grew to know and respect his pa. He cradled and talked to him about things he'd always meant to say one day. And as the dogs became restless and slowly moved away, Jim prepared himself to do the hardest yet the most honorable thing he could for his pa.

THE SOUNDS of the Canada Geese returning, honking across the early morning sky, awakened Jim. The silent winter was over. Life was present again, much to Jim's relief. A southwesterly had been blowing for a week, melting and breaking the ice. Jim never wandered far from the cabin after picking up the last of the nearby snares. His days were alternately filled with deep and lonely sadness or consuming, bitter anger. He was caught in a waiting game - although he ached to leave, he had to be sure all the waterways would be clear of ice.

Jim repaired and sealed the freighter canoes as the March days grew longer and warmer. He sorted their furs, dividing the most valuable mink, lynx and otter into the lead canoe, which he would now pilot. The rest of the beaver and fox furs would follow behind him. Covering the skins with canvas, he tied them securely and prayed they'd make it. He tied the canoes to shore with a double rope to the nearest tree and prepared to wait. The smaller canoe would be stored in the equipment shed.

With that job accomplished, he cleaned the cabin and packed the remainders of smoked partridge and deer meat. The dried fish was almost gone, but now the northern pike was plentiful, and the fresh fish was a welcome treat. He leaned the toboggan against the cabin, his hands running along the smooth birch boards, as he remembered his pa's guiding help.

It was almost a month since he had lowered his father's wrapped, weighted body into the icy lake. He still could not bring himself to sleep in the cabin. It ran warm and cold with too many memories. Sometimes, in the evenings, as the gentle breezes whispered through the budding trees and the campfire crackled and popped, he'd strain to hear his pa talking, his hoarse voice encouraging him to go on. At those special moments, in the warm, comforting space between consciousness and sleep, Jim felt his father's presence, and a healing sense of peace flowed over him.

Jim had absorbed a mountain of knowledge, learning how to read the land and watching for signs of the weather and the animals. Deep down, though, he was afraid. Jim had a long way to go to get back to Ile a la Crosse and the trading post. The water on the Hamilton River would be higher, and the rapids could be more dangerous. He wasn't sure he could make it.

The following morning found him as confused as ever. "I need my pa!" Jim hollered at the top of his lungs, as he had on more than one occasion. His dark brown hair was long now, hanging over the collar of his jacket and constantly in his eyes. At seventeen years of age, he was still quick to anger. And the fear of the upcoming trip made him cross. "Why did you bring me here?" he hollered again. "Why did you have to go and die on me?" He kicked viciously at the woodpile, releasing some of his pent-up feelings. *How could his pa live like this - by himself with no one to talk to for eternal months on end?*

Jim yelled his frustration again. "What was the point of bringing me here?" The land had lost its appeal to Jim. Without his father, springtime lost its usual hopeful meaning. Now it only made him aware of the approaching hazardous journey. Jim barely noticed the forests filling with bright green foliage, the chattering of squirrels, nor the return of vast flocks of snow geese and arctic terns. He was too lost in his own wilderness, both aware and ashamed of the fear that curled in his belly at the strangest times.

Unable to sit patiently, Jim often took the dogs on a hike, hunted for fresh game, or paced the shoreline. With more grit than he thought he possessed, Jim decided to wait another week after the ice had completely left the lake to proceed south.

Finally, after a few nights passed without frost, Jim decided it was safe to leave the camp and head home. Jim waded into the cold water to jump into the heavily laden canoe. Two dogs came with him in his canoe, the other three in the following canoe. They lay passively among the piles of fur, knowing a long rest was ahead. The diary was carefully wrapped in oilskin and secured inside his jacket with the contents still unread. Somehow, he hadn't been able to open it. He was still too angry at himself for not convincing his pa to stay home. He was frustrated at him, too, for deserting him in the middle of nowhere.

He paddled out a few hundred feet, then turned the canoe slightly for his last look at the cabin, basking in the sun on the exposed southern peninsula. He hadn't bothered replenishing the woodpile. All the snares and winter gear had been stored inside the cabin and out of sight.

It already looked abandoned, forlorn. Jim closed his eyes for a minute, picturing the fall days he spent netting, then smoking the fish and game they hunted, then building his toboggan. Jim imagined the campfire's lazy smoke curling slowly upwards. His pa, one foot up on a block of wood, was rolling another cigarette, his cap tipped forward, almost covering his face.

"Goodbye, Pa," he mumbled. He swung the paddle again, gliding through the cold, calm water. Lost in thought, Jim paddled slowly to the southern end of Taylor Arm and downwards along one of the tributaries that would bring him into Clearwater Lake. His mind was full of his father and their winter together. He slowly realized that despite the deep aching pain his father's death caused, he was glad he had come. He came to know and understand him, deepening the love and respect he'd always felt.

His pa had shared his life with him. Together they faced the challenges of the North and surmounted them. His thoughts swirled about, causing him to smile or his chest to constrict. So many emotions mixed up in his heart.

Jim camped early, hauling the canoes ashore and tying them. After starting a fire and feeding the dogs, he settled down. Jim was ready now to read the diary. The opening page was a dedication to his son, from his loving father, with the wish that his last journey as a trapper would be the year he taught his son to be a man in charge of his destiny. With tears in his eyes, Jim read that paragraph several times before he could read further. The purpose of their trip was clear now, and Jim was thankful for his unselfish act.

The opening entries were brief, stating the date, the type of weather, and occasionally a note of Jim's trials. His pa showed his rare sense of humor in some of the ventures he'd helped Jim through, but throughout the entries, Jim could sense his father's pride in having his son with him. Later, there were the odd entries of his frustration with his failing health. Finally, too dark to see, Jim laid the book aside for the morning. He slept soundly, his dogs near him.

With dawn and the movement and whimpers from his dogs, Jim awoke and stretched. Eagerly, he searched for the diary again. He started another fire, made some bannock and tea, then began reading again. The last entries were dated mid-March, and Jim pored over them.

Dennis had finally realized he would not make it home this year. He wrote clearly and with great detail regarding what Jim had to do to get himself back home. He went over signs to watch for as he gave directions on how to portage particular locations that would be different from the fall route. All the time, Jim kept silently thanking his father. With this guide, he had a good chance of making the trip home. His last entry was written with a shaky hand, commending Jim's skills and character, encouraging him to find his way through life.

Jim felt tears sting his eyes as he gritted his teeth. His pa sounded a lot more confident in his abilities than he did. "I won't let you down, Pa - I'll make it home," he promised aloud as he gathered up his dogs and gear, then started paddling southwest to Ile a la Croix.

ALMOST FIVE MONTHS after leaving Beauval to begin the trapping season, Jim returned to the small community with a different perspective. All told, he had sold over two hundred pelts. After paying back the grub stake the Post had lent his pa, he still had over one hundred and twenty dollars left. Friday morning found himself soaking in a hot bubbly tub in a boarding house, contemplating his next move.

No matter how much he enjoyed the past winter trapping, he decided he wouldn't do it again. Most of the pleasure came from pushing himself - challenging the unknown and earning his father's respect. He'd never forget the northland and its treacherous beauty, but he knew he couldn't bear the isolation as his father had. His future had to be elsewhere.

CHAPTER 3

With money in his pocket, a fresh haircut, and new dungarees, Jim felt like a new person. He was no longer a young man, but he was still uncertain about his future. Beauval bustled with people, and Jim warmed to the friendly village after being alone for so long. Brother Wilfred had been genuinely sad to hear the news of the death of his pa.

"I'm sorry you couldn't have had more time with your father, Jim. He was a very private, kind man. Someone we could always count on."

"I know. I learned a lot about him, the land, and his trap lines. I tried to look after him, but he was stubborn as heck. I think he would've liked it if I'd followed in his footsteps, but it was too lonely for me after he was gone. Anyways, I doubt I'll go back." Jim's eyebrows knit together as he struggled to contain his feelings of guilt.

"*Mon Dieu*, that's not why he brought you up there. It wasn't about you taking over his trapline. He wanted to teach you to be independent and think for yourself. He knew it was only a matter of time before you'd be left alone, and he wanted you to be prepared."

"I'm glad he brought me to Taylor Arm. We did everything together. I'd always respected him, but we didn't really know each other. By the time he passed away, he'd turned me into an adult who could look after himself." Jim lifted his chin and straightened his shoulders. "We liked each other, you know?" Jim paused a moment before voicing his fear. "You don't think he'd be disappointed if I never returned to fur trapping?" A hint of hope infused his voice.

"Not at all. Your pa may not have told you in words, but I know he was very proud of you. So, if you're not in a hurry to get back home, I could use some help here for a few months. Are you interested?"

"What have you got in mind? As long as I'm home by mid-July, I could probably help out."

"Have you heard of the Central Farm Program? We've got a dozen families coming here in the fall, all with their forty-acre deeds. The government's offering free land if they come north, as long as they farm it. Most of them are from the old country and know how to work hard. I'm in charge of ensuring enough logs are stockpiled and ready for them to build their homes before winter."

Jim spread his hands out in front of him and raised his eyebrows. "I don't know a thing about logging."

"You don't need to. Pete's been logging up here for years. He has two teams of workhorses that speed things up. All he needs is an extra hand. So far, everybody says they're too busy getting ready to plant their crops. What do you say? You can board at the church. The government will pay you ten dollars a month."

"Why not. Let me sell my furs at the Post, and then I'll

come back. Pete might want to see what kind of worker I am first. Where can I meet him?"

"I'll leave a message with his wife. He'll probably come by and see you within a few days. He can't make the quota alone, so I think he'll be delighted to have a strong, young man to help."

Father Wilfred and Jim wandered over to the rectory, where the priest made chicory coffee and talked about the new government initiative. The promise of free land in exchange for developing farming communities drew the hopeful and people unafraid of hard work. By recruiting the Church and the local communities, the Central Farm Program encouraged them to have the basic materials ready for each family to construct their own home. The average family home measured sixteen by thirty, so falling, limbing, and hauling over forty trees per house was daunting.

Within a few weeks, Jim proved adept at spotting the uniform cedar or spruce trees that needed to be twelve to fourteen inches in diameter and at least thirty feet tall. Preferably the warp in that length would not be more than four inches so that the structures could be as square and airtight as possible. He quickly learned the rhythm of working co-operatively with Pete using a two-person eight-foot saw. After falling the trees, they'd use an axe to limb them, then a team of horses would drag them to the outskirts of Beauval, where they were stored for the newcomers.

"Timber! Get out of the way!" Pete yelled as Jim made his way towards the stream for a cool drink of water.

Jim looked up and saw the spruce heading his way. The wedge they had placed must have slipped loose because the tree was now leaning in his direction. Pumping his arms to propel him faster, he jumped over branches and headed towards another stand of trees. He stumbled over a moss-covered rock and dove into the brush, praying he had been fast enough. The thunderous crash beside him and his labored breathing told him he had survived another near miss.

"Holy hell." Jim dropped his head onto his forearm and struggled to catch his breath. Sweat was pouring off his forehead, stinging his eyes.

"You alright, kid?" Pete ran over to him, his hands searching Jim's body, looking for any injury. "I thought I told you not to leave until the tree was grounded! You could have killed yourself."

"I wasn't expecting it to change direction, and I was thirsty." Jim coughed as he sat up, brushing himself off.

"You haven't learned much in the last few months if you're still making mistakes like that. You're a good, strong worker, that's for sure. But your mind's not on falling trees. You're gonna kill yourself if you don't wake up and pay attention." Peter ruffled the young man's head.

Logging was a tough and dangerous job. Pete didn't want the kid to be a casualty at his young age. Over lunch breaks, he had learned of Jim's hopes to return home and set himself up to make a life for himself and marry his girlfriend, Lucy. After this close call, Pete decided it was time to talk with the young man. "We'll strip the last one, and that'll be it for today. Go get the horses, and then we'll tow these logs outa here."

Returning to the creeks, Jim cupped his hands to drink the cold water to relieve his parched throat. He downed several handfuls as he tried to calm his racing heart. That was the closest he'd come to getting hurt. Pete was right. He needed to concentrate on his work, not on his girlfriend, who was only two days away. Jim splashed water on his face and hair as he tried to cool down and get his head straight.

Walking towards the glen where the horses were resting and feeding, he gained control of himself. He harnessed the two draft horses with their collar and hames, speaking to them gently as he patted and stroked their flanks. Adjusting the backstrap and crupper, he led them back to Peter.

"Nice horses you have."

"Yup. One's from my dad's farm, the other I picked up a few years ago when our neighbor's place went broke. They were heading to Prince Albert by train and were selling everything that wasn't nailed down. I gave them a fair price for it. The chestnut sired a colt last spring, so I'll be training that one when he's fully grown."

"Once I settle down, I'd like to pick up a couple too." Jim cleared his throat as he wondered how to apologize to his mentor. "Uh. Pete? I'm sorry about today. I can't stop thinking about my girl back home. I haven't seen her since last August. That's darn near a year now." Jim grimaced and avoided looking at his boss. "I'm getting itchy feet. I wasn't planning on staying here, I wanted to return home to Big River, but Brother Wilfred talked me into helping him out."

"He has a way of talking people into doing things, that's for sure. Either get your head straight or call it quits. You've done your share. We've already cut and limbed sixty logs between the two of us. Tell Brother Wilfred you're going home. You've made a few bucks with us, but it's time to leave while you're still healthy."

Pete grabbed Jim's shoulder and squeezed it, then patted him. "Think about it. Another close call like today, and you could die before seeing your girl."

"Darn it all, you're right. What am I waiting for? It's time I look after Lucy and our future. She was afraid she'd never see me again even though I promised I'd be back. Another mistake like that, and she could've been right." Jim stuck his hand out and firmly shook Pete's. "Thanks, I've learned a lot from you. Maybe we'll see each other again one day."

"Maybe. Help me put the chains on those logs. After we get them stockpiled, you can talk to Father Wilfred. Life's short, my young friend. Don't waste it."

After relieving the horses of their loads, Jim took them to the corral and fed them. He took a soft brush and groomed them, talking to them gently like Pete had taught him. He pumped fresh water into their trough, then walked towards the rectory, where welcoming aromas reminded him of his hunger.

Brother Wilfred was waving them in. "*Vien t'en manger!* You must be starving. It's almost seven o'clock."

"Pete wanted to haul these logs in tonight instead of leaving them in the bush. I'll be back in a few minutes. I need to wash up before eating."

Pete was laughing with the priest when Jim walked in. He caught the tail end of the episode of Jim running for cover, which sounded funnier now than it actually was. Jim took the teasing well, bantering back and forth with his friend about the day's work. After dinner, Pete and Jim went outside with a cup of coffee and sat on the porch, enjoying the sun slipping behind the horizon.

"So, have you made your decision yet?"

Jim nodded his head in agreement. He realized his thoughts often wandered, thinking about his friends and, especially, what Lucy was doing. He had trouble concentrating on the dangerous job, so it wasn't only himself he was endangering, but Pete too.

"You're right. I didn't want to make a mistake and hurt either of us because my head was in the clouds. I'll finish the week, and then I'll head out. It's time to get back home. I don't know what to do with my dogs, though. I don't know where I'm going to end up."

"I'll take Chimo and maybe one of the other ones. But you'll probably find someone at the Post that could use some trained sled dogs."

"Good idea, I'll do that." Jim slapped his hands on his thighs and stood up, determined to move ahead. "Thanks again, Pete. You've taught me a lot. One day, I'll build a home with Lucy."

"You'll do fine, Jim, as long as you focus on what you're doing. When you check the Post for the dogs, see when you can hitch a ride down to Big River. You might be able to make a trade." Pete stood up and shook Jim's hand. "Safe travels."

～

JIM HAD nothing to compare country life to, but he'd heard plenty. Talking to Pete and Father Wilfred in Beauval made him realize how lucky he was. Their rural community in Big River may not have been the perfect place to grow up, but the families were a tight-knit community for the most part. Not many households suffered from hunger. The land provided most of the basics. Still, not everything could be bartered. Cold, hard cash was necessary, which was the initial reason his pa had taken up fur trapping.

If he'd heard his pa grumbling about the government dole once, he'd heard it a hundred times. Jim supposed he'd been fortunate to be an only child. Many of his friends were from large families that had no choice but to swallow their pride and accept the ten to fifteen dollars a month that would pay for repairs for farm equipment, seed costs, or even the shoes that were no longer fit to be passed down to the next child. Times were tough for all of them, yet the children seldom noticed. They were in the same boat together.

Jim loved joining in the Sunday church services that were the lively social event of the week. Playing with the other kids took a back seat as he grew older. He often sneaked into the back of a community meeting after the service and listened to the adults making decisions they would follow for the coming year.

The granary directors often planned work bees and would set up a schedule for the homesteaders to use. Every spring, the farming co-op would spend a weekend discussing seed prices or what grain would fetch the best market price—oats, wheat, barley, or corn. Conversations on available commodity loans or opinions on the newly regulated soil conservation measures grew louder and livelier when the moonshine flowed. After a pot luck dinner, the fiddles, harmonica, and the rhythm of spoons keeping time enticed the whole community, including the children, to relax and shake off the troubles of their world.

AFTER ARRIVING in his hometown of Big River, Jim sought out the Madsen family on the new chestnut horse he bought from Pete. As he guided his horse down the laneway to their farm, he felt a welcome feeling of belonging. Nothing had changed here. Everything was just the same as it always was in the summer. Fields of golden canola were ripening across the horizon, waiting for the perfect moment.

"My Lord, Jim. Look at you. You're a man!" His surrogate mother, Mrs. Madsen, comforted his lonely soul as she held and rocked him side-to-side. "Your father, is he with you? Did he make it?"

"No, ma'am. I'm glad I went with him, though. He died in the place he loved on Taylor Arm. I was with him when the time came." Jim's eyes watered at the memory and the concern he saw in Mrs. Madsen's eyes.

"Come, come in and have some coffee and something to eat while you tell me about it."

Jim tied his horse to the crabapple tree in the front yard and followed her into his second home. A row of six fresh loaves of bread sat cooling on the counter, its aroma making his mouth water. Watching Mrs. Madsen bustle about making coffee and retrieving boiled eggs from the ice box reminded him of his youth when there were few worries in his world other than school and his daily chores. It seemed a lifetime ago.

Her lively chatter soon extracted the most important details of his trip. Jim glossed over the details of watching his pa's health slowly decline and concentrated on the portages and wild toboggan rides through the brush with his dogs.

"You shot a bear? My God, Jim, you're lucky you came out of that alive!" Mrs. Madsen's eyes were round as saucers, her mouth agape with imagined fear.

"Once my pa yelled at me, I came to my senses and shot him. Pa finished it off with his shot. I was even more frightened when we were skinning and gutting the bear. Pa had put the fear of God in me about predators nosing about after the dinner bell was rung."

"You've certainly grown a backbone in a short period. I'm proud of you, as I'm sure your pa was. Do you want to keep the cabin down the road and start working on the farm? You're part of the family now. You're welcome to stay."

"Thanks, Mrs. Madsen. I haven't made up my mind about what my future will hold. Is it alright if I stay there for a while until I decide?"

"Of course. Why don't you head there and now and get settled? After school, I'll send one of the kids down later with a care package of basics. Bread, butter, eggs."

"That's much appreciated. I have something for you, too. I'll be right back." Jim went outside to his horse and hunted through his saddle bags. He had brought back two white rabbit furs, one for her and one for Lucy. He was sure he'd see it adorning their coats or hats this winter. "Here you go. Something to remember my dad and me. I'm sure you'll find a use for it."

"Thank you, Jim. I'll treasure this. You'll see it on my Sunday best." Mrs. Madsen accepted the soft, supple fur and pressed it against her face. Jim could see the appreciation in her eyes, and he leaned over and hugged her before bidding her goodbye.

As he guided his horse down the road to the only home he ever remembered, he thought about the family who had welcomed him into their lives. He'd never forget their kindness, but he doubted he'd stay there forever as his pa had. Although he wouldn't return to the trapline, he had found a sense of adventure inside himself. He hoped once he and Lucy began a life together, they would look beyond the narrow scope of Big River and explore the rest of the province. Who knew what the future would hold for them?

FROM THE MADSENS, he'd heard of the ongoing tension in town between the local thrashing crews and the southern crews traveling the area trying to steal work as the crops grew closer to harvest. The interlopers took on local jobs, negotiating lower service fees for any farmer desperate to save a buck. He remembered the discussion with Paul Geneaux, whose farm bordered the Madsens.

"You can't blame them, Jim. They're desperate. They have families suffering from the drought for the second year in a row down in the Regina area. They'll lose their homes or land if they don't make some money during harvest. Right now, it's not good anywhere."

"What about you? Are you going to use them?"

"I thought of it. Damn tempting to save a few bucks, but the thought of going to church on Sundays and seeing men I'd turned against sticks in my craw. I couldn't do that. I can't turn my back on the people of Big River. I might change my mind if the economy doesn't improve in the next few years. Right now, I can tighten my belt some and keep going, so I will. But I can't offer you any work, Jim, I'm sorry."

"That's ok. I'll look into picking up work where I can. I've got money set aside, so I'll be fine. I've got other things on my mind I need to look after." After shaking hands with Mr. Geneaux, he considered his options as he made plans to see Lucy. He arranged to borrow a buggy from the Madsens for the next day, and he wasn't about to waste any more time. But first, he needed to see Lucy and hold her in his arms. It had been almost a year since he saw her, and he wondered how she'd changed.

Soaking in a deep tub of hot water, Jim closed his eyes and re-lived his first waltz with Lucy, only last spring. He could still feel her hand on his shoulder, her laughing breath close to his ear. He couldn't wait to see her, to tell her about all the things he'd experienced with his pa. To see if she still felt the same way about him. His future depended on her response.

Jim slowly got out of the cooling tub and dressed in the new clothes he had recently bought. As he checked himself in the mirror, the broad shoulders, short haircut, and trimmed mustache made him look years older than he had just last year. Lucy would be surprised at the transformation. Before he made any more decisions or looked for employment, he had to go and see her.

By lunchtime, Jim found himself outside the Belanger's two-story farmhouse. There was activity everywhere. Lucy's three younger brothers and sisters were feeding the chickens and chasing each other. He looked about eagerly, searching for his love. He caught a glimpse of wavy brunette hair, bending down to pick up a towel from a laundry basket to hang on the clothesline.

Transfixed, he sat there watching her sturdy, slender frame work unceasingly at the formidable pile of laundry. Her skin seemed so tanned against the yellow dress she wore, her flowered apron fastened around her, protecting it. The slight breeze carried bits of a tune she was singing, and suddenly he couldn't wait to see her any longer.

"Luce! Lucy!" Jim called as he dismounted from his carriage and walked towards her. She raised her hand to shield her eyes to see who was approaching. Lucy hadn't recognized the voice at first, but as Jim came nearer, he saw her smile as she recognized him. Lucy dropped the garment she was holding and ran towards him.

"Jim! Is that really you? Look at those muscles you've grown—you're a man now!" Lucy glanced about her, then hugged him quickly. She pulled back to search his face and ran her fingertip over his thin moustache. "You've changed. I like it. I'm so happy to see you. I thought you'd never come back," she said breathlessly, her face flushed with pleasure.

"How could I leave you forever? You're all I ever dreamed

of." Jim replied. "You know I tried to see you before I left, but you were in the hospital."

"I know, Stephen told me." Lucy smiled shyly, again glancing around her. Her brothers and sisters had gathered near them, giggling, pointing, and teasing their older sister.

"*Va t'en!*" she yelled at them. "Lunch must be ready inside. "*Va manger,*" she said again as she scooted them indoors. However, as soon as the children were inside, Lucy heard her mother call her name. She grimaced, knowing what would follow.

"C'mon, let's go," she whispered. She undid her apron, dropped it onto the grass, and scampered up the driveway towards the buggy, giggling. Jim ran alongside her, surprised.

"Lucy! Won't you get into trouble? Why don't you ask first?" Jim questioned as he helped her into the buggy.

"*Etes-tu folle?* Never. You know my parents. They wouldn't let me go out with you alone."

Jim snapped the reins, anxious to put some space between them and the farm. He could hear some angry French admonitions following them, but neither turned to look.

It was a glorious summer's day with the fields full of promise under a cloudless blue sky. A light breeze ruffled the stalks of grain, making them resemble undulating waves on a lake. The sun-warmed fragrance of alfalfa scented the air, and Jim savored the sights around him. Even if there was no one about, civilization was evident in the cultivated fields. Only an hour's ride would bring help - or companionship—how he had missed that sense of connection when he was up north.

Jim shared those thoughts with Lucy. They talked incessantly about the past year, bringing each other up to date.

Eventually, Jim pulled the horse and carriage aside, leading them down to a wooded glen near a small meandering stream. The horses would be content to nuzzle the grasses there while he and Lucy found some privacy. He unloaded a picnic basket and grabbed Lucy's hand.

"C'mon, I've lunch all ready for us."

"You were very sure of yourself, weren't you?"

"I was hoping. But you made it a lot easier by not asking for permission." He led her through a narrow band of cottonwoods to the stream's edge. He spread the tablecloth and organized it, keeping the fresh buns, cheese, and apples in their paper bags. He put their soft drinks in the water to cool and returned to sit beside her.

"I can't get enough cheese and fruit lately," Jim spread his hands, encompassing the food he'd purchased. "I went without them for almost five months last winter. Now I can't get enough of them. I hope you don't mind."

"Looks wonderful," she replied and patted the grass beside her. Jim sat down and reached for her hand. For a few minutes, neither spoke. The gurgling of the stream echoed their happiness. The sun now dropping behind them threw a few shadows about, but they stayed in the heat, enjoying its lazy warmth on them. Jim flopped onto his back, gazing upwards. Lucy soon followed suit, and they lay there, content in each other's company.

"I'm glad you're back," Lucy smiled boldly. Her eyes flicked back and forth from Jim's lips to his eyes.

"Me too. I missed you." Jim lowered his voice, almost purring as he traced his finger down her nose and over her lips.

"Good," she teased.

"Thanks a lot! You could say you missed me too."

"I could," Lucy murmured.

"Well, did you?" Jim rolled over to his side and picked a blade of grass. He ran it across her brow, down her cheek, then down her neck, lingering under her chin, then back up the other side of her face. Watching her skin flush and her breath quicken, he knew the answer before she even replied. "Did you miss me?"

"Maybe." Lucy reached towards him, running her hand on his thigh. She glanced up at his eyes, then quickly lowered them, the tip of her tongue licking her lower lip.

Jim looked at her coquettish eyes, teasing him. He threw the strand of grass aside. "I'll get the answer out of you." He leaned over and began tickling her sides. Just as he knew she would, she became hysterical.

"*Laise-moi donc*," she screamed in between high-pitched squeals of laughter.

"Well, answer me. Did you miss me?"

"Yes, yes—I missed you. Ok?" She responded breathlessly, "now stop."

Jim looked at her. Lucy's tousled golden-brown hair spread about her, and her cheeks flushed with laughter. He couldn't hold back any longer. Jim leaned over and kissed her soft mouth. Her response was instantaneous, her breath quickening as she wrapped her arms around his neck. He ran his hand down her dress, feeling the warmth of her skin through the cotton. His lips traveled down her neck, kissing it hungrily, feeling her pulse quicken.

"Oh my God." He whispered as he tried to pull himself away. He drew back and looked into Lucy's eyes, seeing the passion alight in them. She tightened her arms around him and forced him to return to her lips. As her fingers raked through his hair, and her breasts pressed against his chest, it fired a response in him he'd never felt before. Gently he pushed her onto her back and drew his knee between her legs, sliding her dress higher. He could feel the soft yet muscular thighs beneath him tremble with the same desire he felt.

"Are you sure you're ready for this?" he asked her, watching for any signs of uncertainty.

"Yes. More than anything else. I love you."

"I love you too, Luce." He scooped up the tablecloth and spread it out, deeper into the shadows of the trees, where she joined him, unbuttoning her dress. Her naked body almost unnerved him, but he quickly followed suit. Jim threw caution to the wind and explored every inch of the woman beside him. Tenderly kissing the fading scar from her surgery, he whispered his regret that he hadn't been there to help her through. Her response was quick and urgent. The past was past, and she wanted him now. Whenever he held back, she drew him on.

Soon he was experiencing the heated trails of desire her hands made. Both were eager to hold each other, skin to skin. The touch of her satiny skin next to his sent waves of desire pulsing through his body. His lips traveled downwards to taste her nipples, watching them harden in response, as his fingers drew circles around her navel and explored further into her nest of curls. Her curiosity quickly overcame her shyness, and soon she was exploring the heat of his body, too, both of them murmuring and giggling as the passion between them grew. Inexperienced, they soon discovered the solution to their building desire.

Jim watched Lucy fanning herself, her cheeks still rosy from making love, her left leg still entwined between his. He gazed down at the love of his life, swallowing the knot of emotion that overcame him. A shimmering gleam of their sweat still covered her as she lay there, her eyes closed and her hips gyrating slowly. Lucy was murmuring something he couldn't understand, so he tipped her face towards him. She opened her golden-brown eyes, drinking in his features.

"Are you sorry?" he asked. His forefinger traced Lucy's eyebrow, then followed the contours of her cheek. Jim's mustache had given her a light rash above her swollen, pink lips. He felt himself twitch at the thought of making love again. A low growl escaped him as he began to pepper her neck with quick, tender kisses.

"No, it was wonderful." Her tiger eyes were dancing now, excited that the scandalous dreams she'd been having had come true. Jim was home, and life was good again.

"Yeah, it was, wasn't it?" His fingertip continued a path down her neck, around her breasts, ready to start again. Lucy pulled away from him, gathering her clothes. "Where are you going?" Jim asked, panic evident in his voice. "Are you angry with me?"

"No, no. I'm going for a swim in the creek. I don't want to get in the family way as wonderful as this was." She tossed back at him, smiling.

"Oh my God! I didn't even think about that." Jim whispered as he watched her slipping into the water and swimming. He thought of joining her, then flushed with embarrassment. He quickly put his clothes on and went to the stream's edge. She emerged a few minutes later, the sunlight catching the pearls of water on her perfectly formed flesh, a picture of innocence. They smiled as she slipped back into her clothes, at a loss for words for the moment.

Lucy clapped her hands. "*Bien! J'ai faime.*"

"So am I," Jim replied, and they returned to the picnic and ate heartily, their awkward tension slowly easing. Lighthearted, they teased and laughed the rest of the afternoon away, often touching each other tenderly, still amazed at their feelings for each other. On the way back home, Jim stopped the carriage. Nervously, he proposed marriage. Lucy's eyes twinkled with amusement at his bumbling effort, yet she did nothing to help his unease.

"All this because we made love?"

"Not only because of that. I've felt like this for a long time Luce. I love you." Jim's eyes pleaded his case as his hands ran up her arms.

"Are you afraid my father will run after you with a shotgun?" she laughed.

"No! I want to do the honorable thing by marrying you. What's the matter with you? Didn't that prove how much you mean to me?"

"Of course, *mon cher*. And that's exactly why I'm refusing your proposal. You just feel guilty and think this is what you *should* do." Lucy cocked an eye at him, probably daring him to deny it.

"That's not true" Jim's eyebrows drew together in frustration. "I've had enough loneliness. You're all I ever think about. When I think of the future, you're right beside me." Jim slowed the horses and reached over to grab Lucy's hands. "We're old enough to be married—why not start our lives now?"

"And how will you support me? You don't have a job. I can't just run off and not know what lies ahead. After today, I won't be able to see you often. My parents will make sure of that."

Jim noticed her shoulders droop as she realized the possible consequences of her spontaneous decision to join him. "Your parents can't stop our plans. Don't worry about them. And I've enough money from trapping and logging to get us started."

"Where? And if you can't find work here? Look at the

families around here whose men are forced to leave and find work in the cities." Lucy argued. "What would I do if you left me? My family would disown me if I married you - where would I go while I wait for you?"

Jim was surprised by Lucy's worried outburst and the tears in her eyes."You'd come with me. I'll look after you."

"And go to some strange place where I don't know anyone? Never." Lucy folded her arms, angry now at imagined separations.

"Luce... now look... don't get all worked about something that might not even happen. I'll get on with a threshing crew. I'll come and meet your parents and ask them for your hand in marriage."

"No. Are you crazy? They would rather send me away to some God-forsaken relative than allow me to marry you." She shook her head incredulously. "Don't you understand? *Mon Dieu.* I meant it when I told you that the English weren't welcome at home."

"It can't be as bad as all that. We went to the same school, for God's sake! We all mixed just fine."

"That's not the same. My parents had no choice but to let me go if they wanted me to get an education. Ever since I can remember, they've talked about us staying true to our culture. Some families are okay with mixing, but others like mine are fierce about saving our heritage. They have no choice but to mix with the school and shopkeepers, but when it comes to dating and marriage, forget it." Lucy slapped her knee. "You don't understand."

"I've seen mixed marriages happen. They work. In Prince Albert, where my uncle lives, some churches have both French and English masses. It's not a big deal."

"Maybe not there, but it *is* a big deal here," Lucy said tiredly. She turned her head away from Jim.

"I'm sorry. I didn't realize what you'd have to give up for me." Jim reached and turned her face back toward him so she could see the determination in his eyes. "Trust me, Lucy. We'll make this work."

Lucy dropped her gaze and sighed. "I'd be an outcast. Never being able to visit my brothers and sisters, or having my parents to lean on."

"You'd have *me* to lean on." Silence stretched between them.

Jim could see Lucy's solemn face contemplating the choices in front of her as her fingertip absently tapped at her upper lip. Impatiently, he interrupted her thoughts. "Does this mean the end of us? Before we even start?" Jim's voice held impatience and a hint of disappointment.

"Are you ready to give up on our future? I told you I love you, Luce, and I always will. I want to make you mine."

"I love you too. Otherwise, I'd never have made love with you. I used to daydream about this—the impossible dream. I wondered how we could make a life together."

"Will you think about it? You and I both know how we feel. That won't go away. Will you at least think about it?"

"Of course." Lucy scanned the countryside. "I'd better leave you here, though. The farm is beyond the next ridge. I need to think." She stared at him and smiled, trying to lift his sad face. "We usually go to town on Thursdays, but I'm sure I won't be allowed this week. But I'll visit my sister, Therese, and her family the following Thursday. See if you can arrange to meet me there, alright?"

"Yes. I'll be there - and with good news, I swear it. I'll be working by then, I'm sure."

"*A bientot,*" Lucy leaned to him, kissed him lightly, and jumped down from the seat. Jim watched her walk down the road and hop the fence, cutting across the field to her home.

She turned a few times and waved to him. He sat and watched until the dark-haired girl in the lemon dress melded into the ripening fields. Mesmerized, Jim sat contemplating what he had found and perhaps lost in just one warm, lazy summer's day.

CHAPTER 4

The sour smell of body odor wafted upwards as he lifted another stook of wheat to the wagon. Almost midday, the sun beat down upon the laborers, and sweat flowed from every pore of his body. The whining of the separator slowed and finally halted as the boss signaled for a lunch break. Immediately, Jim strode to the tall ten-gallon milk pails filled with cool water. Grasping a ladle, he drank thirstily and poured another scoop over his head, trying to cool down. He glanced about him, watching workers all over the fields stop and go to their wagons, looking for shade and water to cool themselves.

They would eat too. Not always because the workers were hungry, the heat would drain that need from them, but because they knew it would revive their aching bodies and re-energize them. He crumpled down near the rear wheel of the wagon, trying to find relief from the relentless sun. Dark clouds pressed the horizon, pushing the crew even harder than usual. Thunderstorms could surprise them at this time of year and ruin a season's crops with hailstones as large as crab apples. Jim felt a dash of wind, then wondered if this was the beginning. It could be a short break.

He looked about him at the men he bunked with. The crew seemed to get older by the day, and the older men wizened and exhausted. Tenaciously, they clung to the pace of the younger men, knowing full well the boss was watching their progress. If a man couldn't keep up, he had a warning, and maybe two, then he was gone. Another fresh laborer would appear, anxious to earn the six bits a day.

At every farm, an enormous breakfast of oatmeal, ham, and eggs would await them at dawn. Then they'd break into crews and begin thrashing the grain. Their break for lunch between ten and eleven a.m. would be hearty - usually chicken, beans, and vegetables with huge loaves of bread or a hearty beef and vegetable stew with buns. If the farm they worked on had young marriageable daughters, there would often be extras such as pies and sweets. This temptation would give an interested man an excuse to return and eye up both offerings. Lots of coffee and water to wash it down with, followed by a brief rest, then they would be breaking their backs again for another 6 to 8 hours.

And today would be longer. The crew couldn't afford to take the chance that the menacing clouds would bypass them.

Jim watched a few of the older men slump down near the chow wagon and knew at least one wouldn't make the rest of the day. Jim guessed Matthew would be close to fifty years old. After losing his farm to the bank, he and his family lived in a run-down, three-room cabin on the edge of town. The stooped shoulders mirrored his dejected manner as Matthew struggled to do a young man's job to support his clan. Matthew never spoke much. He did his share alongside the others. But by day's end, there was a desperate look about them as the hot sun, and hard labor sapped their strength.

Jim recognized his fierce determination to keep up with the crew was born from despair. Without work without an income to support his family, his whole reason for living would be meaningless. He'd never accept the dole or pity of the men around him. Stripped of his livelihood, his self-respect was the only thing he could hang onto. Jim unobtrusively watched out for him as often as he could.

"You eaten yet, Matthew?" Jim asked as he slid over near him.

"No. Not very hungry. I ate a big breakfast." Matthew sat with his knees up, arms around them, and his hat tipped forward.

"I'll get you some grub," Jim offered.

"No thanks. I'll get it myself later." Matthew turned his head and ignored Jim's offer.

"Suit yourself. Might not be anything left if these fellas go for seconds."

Matthew turned back and looked at him directly, and Jim hoped his face didn't reveal his concern. His pa and Matthew knew and respected each other, but Jim understood he'd never accept charity from anyone. The older man was exhausted, so when Matthew lowered his head and gave a slight nod, Jim let go of the breath he'd been holding. He pulled himself up and headed for the food.

"Alright. Easy on the beans. I get enough of those when I'm home."

The Boyko family who owned this farm had sent two of their eligible young daughters, under their mother's stern eye, to help distribute the food. Demurely, they served the fare, hoping that one of the threshers would take a fancy to them. As Jim approached again, the elder girl giggled and winked at him, but Jim only smiled politely and got Matthew his grub. He returned with a plate loaded with beef stew, carrots, and potatoes and handed it to Matthew, leaving him to eat in private.

Jim sauntered over to the circle of men, resting beside the thrasher. One of the men tipped his head to the side, indicating someone was approaching. Jim turned to see the big boss, Samuel J. Hodgson, approaching.

"Well, men, the weather don't look too good, does it?" Samuel bellowed. "Damn good thing this is the last farm. We'll be heading towards Debden tomorrow. With any luck, the hailstorm will keep heading northeast." Mr. Hodgson scanned the horizon, then eyed the stooks in the field. "Spencer? How much do ya figure we're getting?"

"About 18 bushels an acre, I figure," Matthew replied, tipping his cap back. "Better than down south, that's for damn sure."

"Just enough to keep everybody going, that's about all," Samuel grumbled. "OK, men. No time to waste. Get the horses and move the thrasher over to the next section. Let's move!"

Jim fetched two chestnuts and found himself working alongside Matthew. It took four horses to haul the heavy thrasher, then another team to bring the engine and the racks. Setting up was sometimes a frustrating, time-consuming task. Lining up the engine to the thrasher with horses wasn't an easy job. The men were working against time and the weather. Jim wished they had newer machinery.

Samuel sat astride his horse, pushing and prodding his laborers to work harder and faster. He was beginning to lose his temper, and insults flew. A wobbly wheel let go, and Hodgson almost flew off the handle. "Who the hell's in charge of these wagons?" he thundered as he jumped off the horse, almost livid with rage.

The closest person, unfortunately, was Matthew. Hodgson pushed him out of the way with both hands. "Bunch of idiots! You! What the hell's the matter with you? You're goddam old enough to know you have to check the machinery! No goddam wonder you lost your farm."

Hodgson ordered Matthew, Jim, and Rene to unhitch the horses and repair the wheel. He directed the rest of the crew ahead, some to begin reaping the next section and others to start bundling more stooks. A tirade of abuse never stopped pouring from Hodgson as he realized how much time he'd be losing. Jim had heard about his legendary outbursts but never experienced one. Hodgson could have left them alone to repair the damage and travel with the rest of the crew, but he chose not to.

The distant rumbling of thunderclouds approaching was becoming louder and more threatening. Everyone recognized the futility of getting any more wheat threshed that day. The storm warnings only aggravated Hodgson further. "Stupid bunch of losers - all of you! What do you think you're doing?" he hollered as Matthew laid his tools down.

"Can't ya see? No use trying to fix that now - it ain't gonna help one bit. Might as well put what we have away and find some shelter."

"Did I tell you to stop? Did I?"

"No." Matthew hung his head but remained still.

"Well, then get your ass back here. All of you!"

"Mr. Hodgson - Matthew's right." Jim began.

"This is none of your damn business, kid. I'm the boss! You do what I say—now fix that goddam wheel." Hodgson shoved Matthew back towards the wagon. Taken unexpectedly, Matthew tripped and fell.

"Hey! I don't care if you are the boss - you shouldn't treat an old man like that," yelled Jim as he went to help Matthew.

"Shut up, kid. Don't you know anything? People like him are worth a dime a dozen. If you want to keep your job, keep your mouth shut and work!" The first crack of thunder exploded about them, increasing the tension around them.

"Go to hell!"

"What did you say, boy?" Hodgson dismounted from his horse and approached Jim, his fists clenching in anger.

"I said, go to hell!" Jim yelled back. "You think you're God around here?" A flying right fist landed on Jim's left jaw, knocking him to the ground.

"As long as you work for me, you're damn right I'm God. Got that straight, kid?" Hodgson growled while his angry eyes glittered. "Now get up, and help that old bastard put the wheel on!"

Jim jumped up from the ground and attacked Hodgson. Unable to control his anger, Jim hit him in the jaw, then again in the stomach. Hodgson retaliated, kneeing Jim in the stomach and slamming his fists down on the back of his neck as Jim curled up in pain. Knocked to the ground, Jim reached out and hauled Hodgson down by his boot. Jim laced him a few times about the head before Hodgson rolled aside towards his nervous horse, looking for his rifle.

"You little sonofabitch, I'll get ya!" Hodgson bellowed as he grabbed his rifle, cocking it.

"Ok, that's enough," hollered Matthew, walking between them.

"Get the hell out of the way," ordered Hodgson.

"Ya shoot the kid, ya go to jail," argued Matthew. "There

are witnesses right here - unless ya plan on shooting all of us."

"Get the hell out of my way," Hodgson growled his warning again.

"Don't be crazy—just let the kid go. He's not worth the trouble." Matthew said.

Jim couldn't believe his eyes or his ears. "You're nuts, Hodgson. To hell with you. I quit." he announced, quietened by the threat of a loaded rifle. "C'mon, Matthew, let's go." Jim grabbed Matthew's arm and looked over at Rene, who had stepped outside the fray, staying neutral throughout. "Are you coming?" Rene shook his head. Then to Jim's surprise, Matthew shrugged his arm loose from his grasp.

"Me either," Matthew muttered as his eyes flitted towards the ground.

Jim looked at Hodgson, who was gloating over the situation. "C'mon, guys," Jim wheedled. "Are you going to let him treat you like a piece of shit? Where's your pride? C'mon, let's get the hell out of here."

"Boy, it's time you grew up. Where are these nobodies going to go? There's no work around here except what I give them. If they go now, they won't be working for the rest of the summer—guaranteed. " Hodgson remounted his horse, a cruel grin snarling his lips. "But you-you're worse than they are. Why? Because you're a fool. You hit me, and that's the end of the line." Hodgson glared at Jim. "There's no work for you around here. I'll make sure of that. And I'm not finished with you." Hodgson leaned back in his saddle and pointed at him. "Watch your back, kid. I'm coming for you, make you understand a few things."

Bewildered, Jim looked for support from Matthew, whom he had stood up for. All he saw was a sad ghost of a man, miserably accepting his role and stripped of his pride.

Embarrassed by the older man's shame, Jim looked aside, shaking his head.

"Go on— get the hell out of here," yelled Hodgson. "Move!"

Jim looked at his two co-workers, then nodded. Strangely, he understood. He didn't like what he saw, but circumstances imposed a different burden for them, one that Jim was thankful he was free of. In their own way, it took as much guts to put up with this kind of abuse as to walk away. As Jim strode briskly towards the barn to get his horse, he heard Hodgson yelling at his crew again, bullying them into submission.

Another crack of thunder ripped its way across the darkening sky, but Jim refused to turn around. Why had he gotten involved with other people's troubles? What good had come of it? He'd made enemies with the most powerful man around. Jim mounted his horse, clicked his flanks, and leaned forward, encouraging him to gallop away.

Minutes later, as the skies opened up and released pellets of hailstones, he dismounted and took refuge in a stook of wheat, pulling his horse as far in as he could to protect him. The ice pellets turned to the size of bird's eggs, and Jim watched the darkness fall upon the farm, obscuring the nearest barn. The increasing winds hurled the hailstones with such velocity that they seemed to be flying almost horizontally. Their impact flattened the rest of the fields, and within two or three minutes, the devastation was complete, as was Jim's future in this immediate area.

Lucy wasn't going to be pleased.

When the noisy hailstorm abated, Jim slipped out of the stook, flicking the hay from his clothes. Checking over his stallion, he spoke softly to reassure him, then remounted. The heavy rain soon soaked him as he traveled home to Big

River, but it was the least of his worries. What mattered more was his broken promise to Lucy. His mind searched for solutions to avoid another possibly dangerous confrontation with Hodgson, but he soon realized only one option was available.

It would've been impossible to live in the same area where Lucy's parents lived. If she were right about her parents and how they'd receive him into the family, there would be constant confrontations, and he didn't intend to start his marriage off like that. He might as well start looking for a new place to call home.

JIM MADE his way to Therese's house and enlisted her help. He went home to bathe and change as Therese made the trip to get her sister on the excuse that she needed help with her daughter. Jim rode to the Madsens to bring them up to date and threw his few belongings together in a backpack. Jim emptied his money belt, stuffed four five-dollar bills into his jeans, and mapped out his new plans as he rode into town and sheltered under an oak at Therese's home. Lost in thought, he didn't hear the girls' approach.

"Jim, are you ok?" Lucy cried as she leaped from the carriage.

"Of course, I'm fine." Jim's face flushed as he knew the pain he'd soon inflict.

Lucy's hand went to his face and traced the bruise along his jawline. "Therese told me you'd been in a fight. What about?"

"Doesn't matter. It was stupid, I guess. But old man Hodgson's not going to let it settle. I guess I'm out of work. Permanently."

"Oh no! What are you going to do?"

"The rain has stopped. Let's go for a walk. You don't mind, Therese, do you?"

Therese shook her head and took his horse to the lean-to before heading inside. As they picked their way down the muddy road, Jim took Lucy's hand.

"I love you, Luce." Jim began.

"I know. I love you, too." Lucy withdrew her hand and slipped it into the crook of his arm, hugging him as they walked. "What are we going to do?"

"I've made a decision. I have to leave and find a job and a place for us to live." Jim saw Lucy's eyes widen in surprise and pulled her to him. He kissed the top of her hair. "It won't take me long, I promise." Jim pulled back and gazed into Lucy's troubled eyes. "I'll come for you, and we'll get married."

Lucy's lips trembled, and her voice faltered. "Please don't go. I'm afraid you won't come back."

"Oh yes, I will." Jim passed his thumb under her eye and wiped a tear away. "Don't worry about that. I love you, sweetheart." Jim kissed her tenderly. "You're the most important person in my life. I'd take you right now—right now. But that wouldn't be fair."

Jim pulled away and stared into her eyes. "I'm not sure where I'll end up or how long it'll take, but I'll be back to get you as soon as I can." Lucy's tawny eyes were full of tears. Her lower lip was trembling slightly, and then suddenly, he crushed her to him.

"I swear to God, Luce, I'll come back. Never doubt it." He kissed her passionately then, smothering her face with tiny kisses, trying to erase her fears. "I'll write you every week, and you'll be able to see where I've been. When I have a decent job and a place to live, we'll get married."

"*Mon amour*, how can I let you go?" Lucy murmured. "I'm so scared you'll forget about me."

"Never! And here, this is for you." He reached into his dungaree pocket to pull out his money clip and gave her the contents. "No arguing. I won't let you refuse it. If I can't come back to get you for some reason, this should be enough money for you to come to me."

"I can't keep this." Her eyes grew large at the sight of the money clip.

"Of course, you can. Give it to Therese and have her open a bank account for you." He shoved the money inside her hand, then pressed it close. "You see? I won't leave you stranded. You're going to be my wife, remember?"

"Yes, I hope so," Lucy whispered, her voice thick with emotion.

"Don't doubt it. Together we'll make a great life. Believe it," Jim tried to lighten the conversation, and Lucy nodded, still somewhat in shock. They held hands as they strolled towards a bench near the creek. Jim and Lucy sat close to each other, talking about their future. Soon, Lucy caught the excitement of the adventure ahead and began planning for the time they would meet again.

Twilight fell, and crickets called to each other. With the cool evening air, birds seemed to come from nowhere to have one last feed on the threshed fields, picking at scattered grains of lost wheat. Soft puffy clouds ringed the rolling horizon. The sky was transformed with the sunset into shades of apricot and melon. The warm bouquet of the fields around them heightened the sense of perfection as Jim savored the peace before him.

The softness of Lucy's skin leaning against his arm nurtured a deep feeling of tenderness and responsibility within him. The timing was perfect. "All I've given you are promises." Jim began.

"Mmhm. And I believe them."

"I'm glad. Luce, I want you to have this." Jim took off the gold ring he wore.

"Oh no, Jim—I can't. That was your father's."

"Yes. It's the dearest thing I own. Now it belongs to you."

Jim watched her put the ring on her finger, noting how large it was, and his heart filled with a strange mixture of pride and fear of their unknown future. "We belong together, Luce—and we'll be married one day soon. Trust me."

"I won't be able to wear it, but I'll hide it—or maybe I could put it on a chain or something. Maybe, I could leave it at Therese's place and wear it when I'm with her." She lifted her eyebrow as she thought of ways to protect their secret.

"I know you'd have some explaining to do if your parents ever saw it, but I wanted you to have something of mine to remind you I'm coming back."

"Thank you. You don't need to give me anything. I know you'll be back." Lucy leaned over and pressed a flurry of tender kisses on his lips, memorizing his taste.

There was no easy way of doing this. He stood up and helped his love to her feet. "I'm leaving tonight. The freight train passes by around midnight, and I'll hop one going south. I'll miss you, ma cherie."

They wrapped their arms around each other, hugging tightly. Their hands roamed as they memorized the feel of each other. Jim kissed his fiance gently, then pushed her away, determined not to prolong the agony of parting. They walked back towards Therese's home, where he left her with a final embrace.

CHAPTER 5

Jim rode his chestnut gelding south of Big River towards Matthew's rental. The northern twilight had settled, and it was difficult distinguishing where he was. Finally, dim light from a small, two-story farmhouse beckoned him to his last stop. Jim knocked at the door.

"Yeah? Oh, it's you." Matthew's eyes shifted away from his protector in embarrassment.

Jim cleared his throat. "Matthew, I'm leaving."

"Smart thing to do. 'Bout today—"

"Never mind. I shouldn't have lost my temper. Anyways, I only came to ask if you could use an extra horse. I can't take him with me, so," Matthew shrugged up his offer.

"A man can always use an extra horse. How long are ya goin' for?"

"I don't know. I'll be back once I get a steady job, though. Got a few things to clear up here once I settle down."

"Mmhmm. Well, yer horse will be here when ya get back. Ya hopping the train?"

"Yeah." Jim was sure his uncertainty echoed in his voice, but it was true that he was nervous.

"Know anythin 'bout that?"

"I'll learn," Jim shrugged.

"Best place to get on and off's on a long corner. Trains slow down for them. Jump before you get to a town. Ya never know how the coppers are at the junctions."

"Thanks. I'll remember that." Jim shuffled nervously, his eyes darting toward Matthew, hoping for more advice.

"Sleep with your clothes on, or the hobos will steal ya blind. Ya gotta knife?"

"Yeah."

"Hope ya won't need it. Desperate men don't fight fair, so remember that." Matthew reached out and shook Jim's hand. "Good luck, kid."

"Thanks."

Matthew came outside and took the horse from him, leading the stallion to a small corral behind the house. No fuss. Jim felt a tiny flutter in his stomach but pushed it aside. He'd left before without knowing what he was getting into and returned alright. He nodded his thanks, turned, and strode away briskly, heading south.

Inexplicably a smile tugged at his lips. *What a feeling!* Young, free, and on the verge of another adventure. Jim would be back for Luce in the spring. He was sure of it. He began to whistle, his thoughts racing optimistically ahead to the future. The miles dissolved quickly as Jim's excitement grew.

He took his pocket watch out and lit a match, trying to gauge the time. He was coming closer to Debden and their grain elevators. 3:10. He had about an hour to get into place on the bend. He picked up his pace, breaking into a slow sprint, trying to cover the remaining seven or eight miles faster. If he missed it, he'd catch a morning one, but he'd rather take this one while it was dark.

Endurance learned from his trapping days held him in good stead. He quickened his pace again as the lonely hoot of a freight train passing the outlying reserve caught his ear. The clear moonlit night outlined the granary and village. Jim's breathing, coupled with the clodding noises his boots made on the gravel road, were the only other sounds to be heard. Jim veered to his left, catching the cooler breeze from the river. Grass rustling against his pant leg threatened to slow him down but to no avail.

Against the moonlight, he saw the beginning of the long snake-like freight train. Pausing for a breath, he scouted the area. The rail lines rose about three feet above the fields and turned south in a long, lazy curve. Laying down in the pasture, he eyed the approaching ride with trepidation. Would it be a full load with no open access to the cars? These days it wasn't likely, although sometimes cantankerous brake men would lock up the empty cars to cut down on hobos hopping the rails. Keeping low, he scanned his rumbling lifeline.

Clackety, clackety, clack. Clackety, clackety, clack. The sound of the metal wheels churning against the rails had a repetitive rhythm that was mesmerizing. The hiss of steam and belching smoke clouded the air, making it resemble a menacing dragon slithering through the night, challenging anything to stop it. Sparks occasionally flew from the rails, and the smell from the overheated metal, mixed with loads of grain, permeated the air. Dust swirled up and caught in his nostrils, making him cough. The night trains didn't stop here. They would head south to the main rail line in Prince Albert and Saskatoon and, from there, branch off.

Indecision made his heart pound, and finally, Jim forced himself to leap. The odd boxcar had a door left partially opened, and Jim spurted alongside the train, waiting for one to pass. Glancing over his shoulder several times, he finally saw his chance. Lunging at the box car, he gripped a metal rung on a side ladder. His shoulder socket screamed in agony as the force jolted his body to the train. Jim tried to find a foothold. Legs flailing, he inched his hand forward, looking for balance, when suddenly he felt a large hand grasp his arm.

"Bloody idiot!" a harsh voice snarled. Startled and still unnerved from his escapade, Jim tried to see who had saved him. The darkness of the cavernous boxcar was all-consuming, and he gave up, collapsing on the rough floor. The shock had knocked the wind from him, and his lungs screamed for oxygen as his heart beat wildly.

He could feel the blood pounding in his ears as he tried to calm down. The air inside was warm and stale, causing Jim to panic. He sucked in gulps of air, but he couldn't catch his breath. Combined with the inky darkness, Jim felt he was suffocating. Would this be the way his life ended? Gasping, Jim lunged toward the door, desperately looking for relief. Again, strong, bony fingers grasped his arm, holding him back.

"If ya woulda waited 'til the mornin', it woulda been a lot easier. Why do you kids try and kill yerselves tryin' to hop the night trains? Dumb, dumb, just plain dumb."

Hearing the voice again had a calming effect, and Jim slumped to the floor, angling his head near the opening. Struggling to regain his composure, he remained silent and tried to even out his breathing. He heard snoring from somewhere further in the boxcar and a grumbling moan from someone closer to him. Calmer now, Jim turned over as his eyes grew more accustomed to the murky shadows. Except for the occasional slice of light from openings near the top of the box, the thick rough-hewn planks kept it dark inside. An unmistakable odor of soiled hay told him that this had once been a cattle car.

Slowly, testing his left shoulder, he hauled himself up to a sitting position. He looked at the man sitting next to him. His weathered felt hat was pulled over his eyes, and his arms were wrapped around his knees, his worn clothing a testament to his present predicament. He strained to see through the inky shadows and saw four other forms. No one else offered a greeting, so Jim assumed they were all sleeping. Now that the danger had passed, his excitement mounted again. The adrenaline gave Jim new energy, and he wasn't ready to settle down for sleep.

"Hey!" Jim waited for his rescuer to answer him. "Hey, you - thanks for giving me a hand."

"Shut up, kid, and go to sleep."

"My name's Jim Taylor. I'm heading east, looking for work." When no comment was forthcoming, he tried again. "What's your name? Where are you going?"

"Damn you, kid—you gonna talk all night?"

"You got something better to do?" Jim saw the glint of amusement as the lined, dirty face looked at him.

"Ya gotta smoke?" the man retorted.

"Nope. Don't smoke." Jim replied. "My Pa used to. I saw him so desperate he'd use dry weeds and mix them with shreds of hemp. Then he'd cough like hell."

"My name's Luther Blackwell. But I go by 'Blacky'. Yer new at this life, aren't ya, kid?"

"Yeah. First time. I used to trap off the Churchill River Basin with my pa. I was kicked off a thrashing job, so I'm heading out. Look for something new."

"Tell ya what, kid. Do yerself a favor and go back trappin'. I mean, look at ya - yer ripe to get the shit kicked out of ya."

"Why? I haven't even done anything yet. And stop calling me kid." Jim could feel his face flush, and he was glad the darkness saved his pride.

"Look at ya. Good boots, good jacket—ya even got a backpack for chrissakes."

"Our neighbor's uncle was in the war and gave it to my pa. Now it's mine. It's only an old canvas thing. Who'd want to steal that?"

"There are men on these trains and in the shanty towns who would kill for yer clothes and a pack like that come winter. Ya ready for that?"

Jim looked at his clothes again and then again at his new friend's. He realized his stupidity at once. "I have a knife to protect myself."

"That's good, and ya'll need it. Ya better not borrow trouble, though. Oh, what the hell—stay with me in the mornin'. We'll leave before the others get an eye on ya. Then we'll hitch back on later."

"Thanks, Luther, I mean Blacky." Jim tried to curb his questions, but he couldn't help himself. "Where will we be?"

"You'll see, kid. Just shut up and let an old man sleep, will ya?"

Jim sighed, his mind racing with excitement. His imagination caught fire as he played through the possibilities this trip could mean for him. Finally, the warming air and the monotonous rumble of the rail cars lulled him to sleep.

"C'mon, kid, let's go." Jim felt another gentle kick to his legs as his eyes opened. "Ssh, quiet. Feel the train? It's slowin' down again. We're near the outskirts of Prince Albert, where the rivers meet. I don't have time to explain. Watch and follow me." Blacky crouched near the opening, looking into the hazy early dawn. Jim could see a lot of shadows, so he guessed they were near trees, probably close to a river. "Ok, kid, drop and roll."

Luther jumped then, and before Jim could stop and think about it, he jumped too. In midair, he realized his plight. With split-second timing, Jim tucked his head between his arms. On impact, his feet slid in the sharp shale, and he tumbled down the rest of the steep bank, landing about twenty feet from Luther.

"Holy hell!" Jim exclaimed as he stood gingerly, testing his ankle and brushing off his clothes.

Blacky stood there grinning like a Cheshire cat. "Least ya do like yer told."

"Maybe I'll think twice next time," Jim shot back. "Wasn't there any better place to jump than that?"

"Sure, there is—two reasons we did it here. First, I had to see if ya had guts and could do what yer told. Second, and most important—about two miles down the track's a shanty town. Most people there are decent people—down on their luck, y'know. But ya got some learnin' to do before ya go any further—unless ya feel like fightin' a lot."

"I'll fight if I have to," Jim replied.

"Sure ya will. But dirty fightin's different than what yer used to, I'll bet. There are gangs of men that'll beat ya up just because they can't stand the sight of ya. Or the coppers and the 'con-cerned' citizens might decide to clear a bunch of us out. Ya ready for that?"

Jim shrugged, trying to look nonchalant. "You made it. I figure I can, too."

"Sure, kid - maybe. Once ya know the ropes, ya make it, or ya get smart and leave the rails. If you live."

"Well, I don't plan on hopping trains for the rest of my life," he shot back. "I'm going to get work. They say there's good-paying work back east – logging and mining in

Ontario and Quebec. I'm young, strong, and willing to work. Won't take me long to get settled."

"Ha. Don't be so cocksure. That's what everybody thinks," Blacky retorted. "Before ya have a chance of that, ya better make yerself a little more invisible. Ya stick out like a sore thumb, kid. Take that jacket off and wash it through the rocks at the river. Beat it up a bit, make it look more worn. And it ain't a bad idea to do the same to yer jeans and hat."

Jim did what he was told. As he labored by the river, Blacky parked himself nearby in the shade of a poplar, then began recounting his experiences on the rails. The summer and fall were the best, Blacky told him. At least you didn't freeze to death. And most outlying areas were decent to the hobos. You could often get good meals for a day or two in exchange for chopping a cord of wood, repairing fences, or other such work. An unspoken agreement existed between the hobos and the farmers. Never ask for more than your food and shelter, then, you could stay a few days. After that, you moved on. The rural families had enough hardships without adding a permanent addition. While the hobos weren't welcome with open arms, at least they were treated with compassion.

Blacky told him of a place slightly east of Winnipeg, Manitoba, that kept him over a month in the dead of winter during his first year of traveling. Half frozen and starved, they fed him and nursed him back to health. The Ukrainian had even mended his shoes while his wife knit him a pair of socks and a vest. However, as soon as the weather warmed, he was kindly sent on his way with a large brown bag lunch.

Now, if he were out of work and on the rails again by November's end, he'd head for one of three good hobo camps he knew of, where there were tight-knit co-operatives and plenty of firewood. He came in, emptied his pockets, and shared a winter with them. Those that could work did and brought home supplies. Others would hunt, fish, or sneak into the city to beg or steal what they could. And always, their ears would be open for news. Good or bad.

Both news would likely come from the same source, the 'Christian' community. The *Sally Ann* would entice people to listen to the word of God by giving them food, while the women and children sometimes got shelter or basic schooling. Blacky figured it was a fair trade-off. Each side got something. But then, eventually, if the community were hard-pressed financially, a group of men would come out, rousting them from their make-shift shelters and forcing as many as they could down the line. *They had to look after their own first, don't ya know?*

Jim finished washing his clothes to Blacky's satisfaction and spread them to dry. He retrieved a hook from his tin of essentials in his backpack, caught two small pikes, and cooked them over a small fire. The smoky, tender fillets quietened their stomachs, and he could concentrate again on his survival lessons.

"Ok. Saskatoon, Sault Ste. Marie and Clearbrook are all good spots. I don't think I'll need them, but it's good to know."

"And just tell 'em Blacky sent ya. Blacky from Lethbridge. Got it?"

"Yeah. Now, what about the bad places? Any place I should stay clear from?"

"Port Arthur, fer sure. And Windsor - cause it's too close to Detroit, and that's a rough lot there. And if I don't have to go through Toronto, I don't. In those places, yer back ain't safe from nobody. The coppers would just as soon shoot ya rather than let ya board a train. And most of the hobos there are plain mean. Ya ever thought about hell, kid?"

"Sure, hasn't everybody?" Jim retreated a few feet as he saw Blacky's eyes harden.

"Well, that's where ya can find it. See, some shanties are too close to the big city, and bein' so close to people who have a real life can make some hobos bitter. They'll do almost anything for a bottle of booze or a few bucks to feed their family and make life bearable." Blacky ran his fingers through his hair, then rubbed his whiskers as he remembered. "If ya wanna see people with nothin' left, and I mean nothin'—go to Windsor. Ya see it in their eyes, in the way they move. There's no hope left in them, just cussin' and fightin' and hate. Ya won't find me anywhere near a big city. Life's tough enough without seein' that."

Jim could barely imagine the despair Blacky described. The picture of human misery swelled to capacity on the edge of existence seemed too cruel for this earth. "Why doesn't somebody do something?" Jim barked. "It's not right."

"No, kid, it's not. But that's the depression for ya. I heard tell even the rich are sufferin'. Some even killin' themselves 'cuz they can't stand the thought of bein' poor. Heard tell they're the ones that caused all this shit—an' if that's true, they oughta be sufferin'."

Jim nodded in agreement. Blacky knew a lot about the politics of the land, something Jim had never paid much attention to. His whole world revolved around the immediate concerns of central Saskatchewan. He had never thought about its relationship with the rest of Canada. He was beginning to see problems from a new perspective. "So, how long have you been riding the rails?"

"Since 'bout March of '30. I used to work for a cattle ranch that went broke. My brother was a bookkeeper in Calgary. I went and stayed there awhile." Blacky lowered his head, shaking it as the memory overcame him. "Watched him grow old within months—I'll never forget it. Anyways, I left."

"That's over eight years—and you've never found a place to settle down?"

"Could've, I guess. Never wanted to. I've crisscrossed the prairies to Quebec and back at least four, five times, and I like it. I work when I can, and then I move on." He raised an eyebrow at Jim, almost apologetically. "Guess the rails kinda got in my blood."

"But don't you get lonely? Don't you want to settle down?"

"What for? An' let the banks take yer house, or yer land again? Look at all 'em people that busted their ass—and for what?" Blacky shook his head from side to side. "Nope, not for me."

Jim's eyes narrowed at the thought, then shrugged his shoulders, almost overwhelmed by his reasoning. He didn't know why it should matter to him that Blacky had given up. "So, you quit? Gave up?"

"Look ya little shit, ya don't know nothin' yet, do ya? So shut up. We'll see what ya gotta say after yer outa work for a while, eating soft potatoes and beggin' for beans." Abruptly, Blacky stood up and strode down the river bank, his hands shoved inside his worn dungaree pockets.

Damn, Jim thought. The first guy who's tried to help me out, then I spit in his face. He scrambled up and hollered for him to wait. Blacky turned, pointed, and told him to sit still. He'd be back. Rebuked, Jim watched the retreating figure disappear around the river bend.

CHAPTER 6

The first few months Blacky and Jim traveled together had been as exciting an adventure as Jim had wished. He grew adept at judging a train's speed and hopping a ride. Jim also learned to jump backward off a train when the terrain was steep, tucking his head into his chest to lessen the risk of breaking his neck. He knew he was fortunate to have Blacky with him, explaining the routes and introducing him to the regulars on the line. They worked a few days to a few weeks whenever they could, yet steady work had eluded them. It wasn't until they crossed into Ontario that tension crept into their lives.

The CN Railway enforced security more closely here, and as Blacky had forewarned, there were some miserable sons of bitches around. It seemed like their attitude rubbed off on everyone. The hobos they encountered looked tough and kept to themselves. Some were visibly afraid of newcomers and preferred to stay in the shadows. Thanks to Blacky's reputation, the bullies left them alone. But nobody could predict where or when they'd run into the Big Ox or

Mad Marvin, two of the meanest rail yard guards around. It made everyone edgy.

Jim volunteered to scout the rail yards in Kenora, his youth and speed the logical choice. If the coast remained clear, Blacky would follow. Since approaching the larger cities where more security was taken, his keen sixth sense had saved their skin more than once. Yet...

"Ok, Jim—coast's clear. Go!" Blacky whispered.

Dawn was edging over the horizon, easing the shadows that hid the myriad of train tracks. Jim ran from the brush cover across the several sets of empty rails in the yard towards the lines of idle trains. He glanced about him as he ran, looking out for Mad Marvin. He and Blacky had enough of this crazy area and were moving on.

Blacky prepared him with a description and warned him to beware of Marvin. Perhaps the gun gave him the stature he craved, Blacky explained, because his 5'4" skinny frame would otherwise not scare anyone from trespassing. Whatever the reason, Marvin enjoyed the power his gun gave him, which was dangerous.

Jim later wondered how he missed seeing him. True, it was sunrise, and maybe the sun blinded him, blocking his approaching form. Yet, all he remembered was hearing him yell.

"Hey, you! Stop right there."

Stunned, Jim stopped in his tracks, gulping in the air to calm his breathing.

"What the hell do you think you're doing here?"

"Nothing, sir. Just passing through."

"This ain't no goddam public road. This railyard is private property. Didn't you see the signs - No Trespassing?"

"I saw some signs, but I can't read," Jim lied. He could see by the sneer on the guard's face that he was in big trouble.

The guard spat a wad, wiped his mouth on his sleeve then continued chewing snuff. His beady brown eyes glared at Jim. He could feel the loathing emanating from the guard like ripples in a pond.

"Can't read, hey? Well, I'm telling you to get the hell off this land. Take the road like the other bums around here and move on. We don't want the likes of you around here."

Jim's eyes skimmed the area, checking out his position. The hiss of steam and the slow growl of wheels turning caught his attention. To his left, the second train over was sluggishly moving forward.

"Well? What'cha waiting for? Move it!" Mad Marvin patted his holster. "You better move it, kid, before you get an invitation here from my buddy."

Jim looked around for Blacky—what should he do? "What's it to you if somebody hops the rails? It doesn't hurt anybody." Jim began, inching his way left.

"Says who? Nobody gets a free ride around here, kid. The railways are a business, and if you want to ride it, you buy a ticket and ride the coach." The guard stepped closer to Jim and growled. "I ain't got time for your bullshit. Now get going before you make me mad."

Jim saw a familiar figure behind Marvin scampering between the idle trains and heading towards the rolling boxcars. Suddenly Jim lunged toward Marvin, catching him off balance and sending him to the ground. He jumped lithely over the tracks and headed for cover. Jim could hear Mad Marvin scrambling to his feet, cursing a mean streak. He heard a shot fired and a split second later caught its spark as it hit the metal coupling between the box cars. *Holy shit*, Jim thought frantically. A glance over his shoulder proved that the guard wasn't finished with him yet. One angry security officer was chasing him.

The train was rolling along nicely now, picking up speed. Jim had difficulty keeping his balance as the ground was crisscrossed with gravel and changing rail lines. The noise level was high, the clamoring of the wheels echoing against the idle cars on either side of it. He could hear some shouting, but he couldn't make out any words or directions. He looked up and saw a figure several box cars ahead waving to him. A whistle blew, and as a box car handle slid past him, he burst forward in a desperate attempt to grab it. His calloused hands gripped the metal as his feet scrambled to get a hold, his body swaying with the rhythm of the train. He heard a burst of gun shots.

"Ow! Dammit!" Pain knifed its way up the arch of his foot. Panic mixed with fear gripped him. He'd been shot. Struggling to keep his balance, Jim managed to inch his way to safety. Once inside the rail car, he sat down and raised his foot over his right knee. Blood was seeping out of a neat half-inch hole. The exit hole was more significant, and the burning sensation in the meat on the side of his foot told him he was lucky. The bullet had probably entered at an angle while he was swinging. Jim hoped it was a flesh wound with no broken bones to mend.

Jim checked out the compartment. Thankfully, he was alone. Jim took off his jacket and removed his shirts. Taking his boot off slowly, the beads of sweat quickly formed on his brow from the throbbing pain. He wrapped his worn cotton undershirt around his foot and tied it as tight as possible. He slumped against the boxcar wall, barely aware of the splinters penetrating his bare skin. Worn out from the escapade, he made no effort to re-dress himself. Instead, he closed his eyes and forced his mind to relax as he concentrated on controlling his breathing. Jim wondered if he would ever find a place to settle or if he'd turn into another desperate soul like his friend.

BLACKY MADE his way along the boxcars, leaping expertly from one to another until he found the one Jim occupied. As he entered, Blacky noticed Jim's exhaustion and was pleased to see that the kid had the brains to look after his foot first. The bloody shirt was already soaked, and as he watched, Jim shuddered. Blacky covered the kid with his jacket and sat down to plan the next move.

The kid was lucky. No doubt about it. But it was the kind of luck that followed courage. Blacky decided they'd stay on the train as long as possible and get as close to Sault Ste. Marie as possible. With a foot like that, Jim wouldn't be traveling for a while. They may as well hole up for the winter.

THE FIRST THREE weeks found him almost totally dependent on Blacky. Without proper medical supplies, Jim had succumbed to an infection and subsequent fever with his wounded foot. Depending on others to do his share of community chores grated on Jim's pride. Bathing his wound in salted water and drying it carefully eventually allowed him to walk about with a hand-hewn cane. Within a month, he accompanied Blacky outside the camp, looking for day jobs or bringing home firewood or anything else that could help. They moved on as rumors of steady work filtered down the rail line.

Almost three months later, Jim entered the small general store outside Sault Ste. Marie carefully doled out five cents for two sheets of paper, an envelope, and a stamp. He was becoming a regular here ever since his foot healed. The camp on the outskirts of Sault Ste Marie was friendly, and they were warmly received. But now, Jim and Blacky were getting anxious, waiting impatiently for the cold snap of winter to lessen its grip on the land before they continued.

"Any mail for Jim Taylor?" he asked the postmaster.

"Nope. Only local stuff this week. Persistent, aren't you? You've been here every week for months now, and you haven't got anything yet, have you?"

"No, sir. Maybe this week, though." Jim replied politely. No use making enemies and telling him to mind his own business. "Can I borrow your pencil, please?"

Jim noticed the postmaster eyeing him up and down. He made an effort to present himself as neat and clean as possible so that the kindly man would offer him work. Jim thanked him as the storekeeper reminded him sternly to return it promptly.

Jim nodded and sat on one of the stools surrounding the potbelly stove. Warming his chilled fingers, he wondered again why Lucy hadn't written him. He should've had something by now. Had she forgotten him already? He wrote in small neat letters, trying to cram in as much as possible on a sheet of paper. Jim told her about the camp and the friends he'd made, emphasizing that he was moving when the weather warmed. He reminded her of his promise to create a new life for them both, then begged her to please, *please* write him. Mission accomplished, he addressed the letter and pushed it through the mail slot.

"Here's your pencil back. Got any jobs you need doing?" Jim raised his eyebrows and offered a pleading smile.

"Ah—what the hell. Fill up the barrels and bring in another load of wood for the stove."

Jim checked the barrels and went to the storeroom. He hauled out a sack of beans, a couple of bags of oatmeal, and a jug of salted pickles. After filling the barrels, he went outside, chopped an armful of kindling, and brought in two loads of firewood.

"That's good enough, Jim." the postmaster said. He took out a brown paper bag and threw a few scoops of beans inside. He tossed in an onion and then went behind the meat counter. He wrapped a slab of salt pork in brown paper and added it to the bag.

"Thanks a lot, sir," Jim said as he lowered his eyes to the bag. A lump stuck in his throat. Charity was still hard to accept, yet for the good of the camp, he swallowed his pride.

"And don't go telling the others to come around. I'm not going to be handing out for every Tom, Dick 'n Harry."

"No, sir. I understand. I'll be by next week. If you hear of anybody needing help, could you tell them about me? I sure could use some work."

"You and fifty other men around here. But sure, I'll keep an eye out."

Jim nodded and thanked the storekeeper again. He tucked his groceries inside his jacket and left the warm confines of the store. Outside, the bitter cold attacked him. He shivered and hugged his coat closer, turning the collar up and thrusting his hands into his pockets. After making his way carefully across the icy, wooden walkway. Jim crossed the road, his boots crunching through the packed, crusty snow. The slight limp was no longer the result of the wound; it had long since healed but from an effort to keep his foot up off the cold ground. The aching, chilling numbness the cold caused hurt almost worse than the bullet ever had.

Looking about him, Jim felt a sense of despair overcome

him. Even in the north country, he had never experienced this misery. Much as he hated to admit it, he had lost Lucy. She should have written him by now if she still loved him. No doubt her parents pushed her to meet other young men, and she probably moved on. Yet, his heart couldn't shake Lucy's indifference and the fact she didn't have the decency to tell him. Without her connection, he felt lost. Except for Blacky, he was among strangers. True, some of them were kind, but still, they were strangers in an unfamiliar province.

He thought back to the beginning of his trek, amazed at his naiveté and his sure sense of optimism. The camp appreciated his expertise in setting traps for wild game, but Jim still had difficulty accepting their plight, no matter how much better his presence helped them. Nestled among the giant fir trees, families constructed shacks of every description for shelter. The trees offered refuge from the bitter winds, and the rain beat less vigorously on their roofs of tar paper, planks, and scavenged canvas. The abundant firewood kept the chill down, so the smoky haze they breathed was a small price for the warmth it gave.

It was, by most standards, a good camp, but in Jim's eyes, it overflowed with hopelessness. Like the people who inhabited it, it had no sense of optimism. It had no—*color*. Everything was grey, brown, black, or dirty white. Even the children's faces had no joy, only a questioning sadness. He hoped that despair would disappear once spring arrived, but it seemed a long time to wait. Jim shook his head, trying to dispel his mood, but it wouldn't leave him.

He had to leave this place. It was time to head out, whether or not spring had arrived. Even the thought of leaving his best friend wasn't enough to deter him. With that decision made, his heart lightened, and his pace quickened.

"DAMN FOOL IDEA, KID, TRAVELIN' at this time of year. We'll be lucky not to freeze our nuts off," said Blacky as he sat back-to-back with Jim, trying to keep each other warm.

Jim laughed uneasily. It had been more difficult than he imagined hopping a train when the snow and ice hugged the tracks. A slip could mean their last mistake. Once inside, the icy blasts of wind penetrated every crack sucking every bit of warmth from them.

But, Jim was on the move again. Free this time from every tie to his past. He vowed to forget about Lucy and get on with his life.

"So, where do you think we should go, Blacky?"

"Somewhere warm be nice, but we ain't welcome down in the States. They got too many of their own on the lines - they don't take kindly to foreigners coming down either."

"We could go to B.C." Jim offered.

"Headin' the wrong way now. And it's too bloody far to go at this time of year. If it was springtime, then sure."

"Why don't we go into Toronto or Montreal? We might get lucky and find work there."

"Don't you remember nothin'? It's tough in the big cities."

"Yeah—but it's alive. I'm dying of boredom here. C'mon, Blacky, let's give it a shot."

Blacky quietened as he eyed Jim over. "I'd never taken ya there when I first laid eyes on ya. Maybe it would work out now. Ya gotta see for yerself, I guess."

Jim chuckled. Blacky was almost twice his age, and although his tall, blustery looks would scatter many vagrants away, Jim knew he had won a soft spot in his heart.

"I don't know French, so I ain't goin' to Montreal. We'll

keep going 'til we hit Kingston, 'cause I ain't living in Toronto either. Maybe we'll get lucky and get some work unloadin' at the warehouses. We'll have to hit a *Sally Ann* and get some warmer clothes, though."

"We can do that. You'll see, life will be better once we get steady work."

"Alright. And spring's not far off. We can try stevedoring when the ships come on the Lakes again." Although their plan was half-baked, it was a start, and both had a lot to think about as the rolling chatter of the train continued.

Blacky plotted the way carefully, weighing the pros and cons of each city they went through. Jim knew he was still trying to protect him from the more brutal elements. They became as close as brothers, creating a tie they'd both missed. Jim knew he looked upon him as an innocent, always believing better times were ahead. But, as far as Jim was concerned, it was the only way to live. Without hope, without an inner compass, what chance did they have? The road was plenty long and dark as it was.

CHAPTER 7

"You, and you! And the two Wops over there." The foreman's forefinger identified his choices and then pointed them to another fellow marking names down on a pad of paper. "Go on, get the lead out! The rest of ya can move on. That's all we need for now." Hardened by time, he turned and walked away from them, their mumbled pleadings of disappointed men gone unnoticed.

Jim turned and gave the thumbs-up sign to Blacky. They'd been fortunate since coming to Kingston. Sharing a two-room apartment, the two friends scrounged enough work to live decently. Poorly, but decently. They pooled their resources, cooked on a two-burner hot plate, and slept on lumpy mattresses. But when they had a good week, they forgot their problems and painted the town red on the weekend. There was laughter in their lives again, and that alone was worth the price they paid.

Jim hoped he wouldn't be stuck down the hole again. The ship's belly was a humid and airless pit in a Kingston summer. The foreman usually sent the younger, stronger men down there, although it was no guarantee that even they wouldn't suffer heat exhaustion and need to be hauled out. Piece loading timbers demanded endurance, as well as strength.

"You're Jim, aren't you?"

"Yeah."

"Ok, Down the hatch."

"Yessir." Damn. Jim drew his last breath of fresh air for the morning and cursed his luck. He'd sweat off a few pounds today. The only good thing was that time flew by fast. The pace of stacking timbers was like a two-step waltz - dodging PeeVees and guiding the heavy timbers into condensed solid piles, layered into wall-to-wall flooring. The cargo was less likely to shift in heavy seas when loaded that way, and the men needed to pay particular attention to cross-hatching in the hole. Later on deck, the same procedure was used to fill every available space, then lashed down before the freighter left port for open seas. Jim's quick eye and strong back hadn't gone unnoticed, so it wasn't unusual for him to get a shift most mornings. He stepped onto the gangplank, and the smell of cedar rose, greeting him. Hours later, a whistle blew, and Jim finished setting a timber into place.

"C'mon, kid, let's go up." Alberto tapped him on the shoulder, and Jim nodded.

"Wonder if that blonde will be at the coffee wagon today. I haven't seen her for a while." Jim replied, eagerly running in front of his co-worker.

"Maybe. Hot little number, that one. Ya lookin' for some nookie?"

"No, of course not." Jim blushed.

"Sure, sure. Might as well admit it. Yer just as horny as the rest of us here – ya want to see what kind of sweater that honey has on today."

Jim laughed, wiping the sweat from his brow. "Well, I'm sure not blind - but she's nice too, y'know."

"Yeah, real nice. Nice for a price," Alberto snickered, waggling his eyebrows up and down.

"Get off it. She's friendly, that's all." Jim defended.

Alberto's heavily accented voice taunted him. "Don' tell me those blue eyes of hers sucked you in? Did she blink those big eyelashes at you, then look away?"

"You can't fake a blush," Jim defended again, his temper rising.

"You ever see her blush? I haven't."

"Well, I have." Jim retorted.

"Well, maybe she's got the hot pants for ya."

"Why don't you shut up a while." Jim replied disgustedly, "She's not like the hookers on Ontario Street."

"Sure, kid."

His nickname had stuck here too. Jim left him and walked up to one of the taps that served as drinking fountains on the dock. He splashed his face and hands with tepid water, then slicked his hair back as best he could. He dug into his pocket and got a quarter out. When it was his turn to get the coffee and sandwich, Maggie was very busy and didn't have time to make small talk. Men jostled about him, trying to get their lunch before the short break was over. There wasn't even a smile on her face today. Feeling dejected, Jim sat on the pier, viewing the food wagon while eating his lunch and planning his next step.

He watched her handle the coffee and food orders. As the crowd thinned, he saw her scan the small group of men. Her boss called her, so she helped him put the condiments away and pull up the counter, ready to move on to the next dock. Jim kept his eyes glued on her, and as they were leaving, she turned and waved. He smiled widely and stood up, waving back. His heart thumped for several minutes after as Jim tried to ignore the teasing from his fellow workers. Tonight, he'd walk over to her place and ask her out.

He was tired of the casual flings he'd had now and then since arriving in Kingston. It had filled a need and even taught him a few things, but now he was ready for something more serious. Blacky seemed content enough with a day-to-day existence, working, playing poker, drinking, and occasionally getting lucky with the ladies. But Jim needed a relationship beyond that.

The whistle blew, ending their lunch break and interrupting his plans. The afternoon raced on, and by 6:00, quitting time, his shirt was soaked with sweat. Once topside, he undid the buttons, letting the fresh breeze from Lake Ontario cool his heated skin. He'd be back tomorrow, more than likely here, as this ship was still only half full.

"Get that goofy look off yer face, kid, or all the hookers will follow ya home." Alberto teased as they walked up the docks together. "Though come to think of it, maybe I should go with ya—I could pick up yer leftovers."

"In your dreams," Jim quipped back. "You'd have to pay double to get a girl into your bed. And even if I were in the market for one, I'd do better without a Wop beside me." Jim stuck his head under the water tap again to cool off.

"Ha. Y'know us Wops, we know how to make a lady sing." Berto raised his eyebrows suggestively several times.

"Sure 'Berto, sure." Jim laughed. He ran his fingers through his hair and then slapped his hat back on his head.

"Hey, are ya going to the game later at Harry's?"

"No, I'm planning on having better things to do." Jim briskly walked towards his boarding house as Berto lagged behind him.

"Blacky goin'?" Berto yelled.

Jim turned and shrugged. "I don't know. Probably though. He's made a couple of shifts this week, and it's Friday. Figures he's luckier on Fridays."

"Well, tell him I might be going up for a while. See ya later, maybe."

"Sure 'Berto. Take it easy." Jim waved then turned left as Alberto turned opposite at the gate, each heading home.

Jim wondered if Blacky had made a crew today or not. Things were very competitive these days, but his strength was often overlooked because of his age. He pretended it didn't bother him, but Jim had noticed a change in him in the past couple of months. He didn't seem so optimistic. Oh, he drank and partied just like before, but something behind the good times made it look forced. Something hidden behind those once flashing coal eyes.

"HEY, BLACKY. BLACKY?" Jim called as he entered their apartment. The radio was on, and Jim shook Blacky's shoulder. Then Jim noticed the empty pint of whiskey lying on the floor beside him and let him go. He might as well let him sleep awhile. After showering in the communal bathroom down the hall, Jim returned ravenously hungry. He looked inside the ice cabinet and pulled out a carton of eggs and a hunk of sausage. Soon the smell of frying onions and slices of Italian sausage woke Blacky up. He sauntered over, eyeing up the concoction, as Jim poured the eggs over the top. The stale, sweet smell of liquor hung about him as he rubbed his whiskers absently.

"Looks terrible," Blacky growled.

"Grab yourself a plate. It tastes better than it looks." Jim offered as he slowly turned the bubbling omelet.

"I'm bloody sick of sausages," Blacky growled again. "What I wouldn't do for a thick Albertan T-Bone steak."

"Only place you'll get that's back home." Jim divided up the skillet and sat down, cutting each a thick slice of bread to eat with it.

"Yeah, well, I'm almost ready to go," Blacky continued as he picked at the food on his plate.

"You've been saying that all summer. Did you hear about the poker game at Harry's tonight?"

"Yeah, I heard. Some fancy pants wants to play." Blacky joked as he rubbed his whiskers.

"Are you going?" Jim hoped he'd go and enjoy an evening out and get out of the funk he was in.

"I only got fourteen bucks left, kid. And I gotta give you a fiver for the rent tomorrow."

"Forget it. I've put in a lot of hours this month. I'll cover it." Jim picked up the dinner dishes and put them in the sink.

"No way, I pay my share." Blacky's surly voice was unusual.

"Forget it. Don't argue with me. I owe you plenty. Go tonight and break'em."

Blacky shrugged. "You gonna play too?"

"No, I'm going out tonight." Jim couldn't hide his excitement.

Blacky laughed knowingly. "Time to get laid, eh kid? It's been a while, has it?"

"I'm going out to see a girl, maybe take her to the movies." Jim smiled nervously and shrugged his shoulder. "If she'll come with me."

"Right. If ya strike out, c'mon up and see how the games are goin', ok? Ya haven't come up in a long time."

Jim was too cheap to play poker, and Blacky knew it, but

he still liked to have him around. Jim didn't mind. It was fun to have a few drinks with the fellas, and when Jim did accompany him, Blacky always did better. ' Of course, Blacky didn't drink as much then either, knowing that Jim wasn't crazy about him getting soused.

"Yeah, Ok. I'll go up. I don't imagine things will get rolling 'til after eleven or later anyway." Jim grabbed his hat and the light jacket he kept for special occasions, then gave the two-finger salute to his friend. "Good luck."

"To you too," Blacky snickered.

Jim left the apartment with mixed emotions. He was worried about Blacky. He wasn't the dependable, happy-go-lucky guy he used to be. *The booze had gotten to him.* Jim was satisfied with his life, but he could see that Blacky wasn't. He was only here because this was what Jim wanted. Maybe, he should give in and leave town with him, hit the rails, and find another place.

Jim almost bumped into Verella, the old lady who hocked vegetables on their block. "Stupido!" A tirade of Portuguese followed him as he excused himself and continued northeast to Wellington Street. His mind abandoned Blacky and filled instead with the images of a good-looking blonde. He'd checked her out with some local shopkeepers who knew Maggie's family well. Her home was only a few miles away, in a four-plex brick building. In this European melting pot, neighborhoods stuck together like glue. Italians and Portuguese, Finns, Poles, and Jews had their distinct territory, leaving the English and French to themselves. Yet, no matter where you went, you usually felt welcome. Life was tough enough. It helped to keep things friendly.

"Is Maggie home?"

"Who's calling?" A tall, thin man inquired icily. His spectacles sat mid-way down his upturned nose, almost making Jim want to reach out and push them back up.

"Jim Taylor, Sir."

"I see. *Margaret's* studying right now."

"May I see her for a few minutes, please?"

A sigh of exasperation escaped the thin lips. "I'm Margaret's father. I'm not accustomed to men announcing themselves for my daughter's attention without a proper introduction."

"But sir, I haven't been here very long, and I don't know many people here."

"Just as I thought—another vagrant."

"No, sir. I have an apartment on Melrose Street and work nearly forty hours a week, stevedoring on the docks."

"Father?" Maggie arrived at the door, peering around him. "Father, it's ok, I've met Jim before. The grocer at Lee's introduced us."

Mr. Browning's face assumed an air of ill-concealed resentment as he opened the door wider to let Jim in. "You have studies to finish, my dear, but you may have a half-hour break." His language sounded stilted and formal to Jim. He could hardly believe that people spoke that way in real life.

"Thank you, Father." Maggie opened a leaded glass door to the parlor and led Jim inside.

Jim removed his hat, nervously turning the brim in his hands over and over again as he glanced around him. He didn't expect to find such a fine collection of crystal and china from the plain, unassuming exterior. The settee covered in a fine, handsomely crocheted throw almost looked too delicate to support two grown people. Maggie turned on a lamp that threw pinpricks of light through the shade rimmed with dozens of prisms. Shelves and more shelves covered two walls, and it seemed to him that every possible inch contained something fragile.

"Don't be nervous," Maggie smiled.

"I'm going to break something. I can feel it." Jim's low voice cracked as he responded.

"Don't be silly. Please, sit down and relax. This room's rather intimidating, isn't it? I think that's why Father keeps it this way."

"It sure makes *me* uncomfortable. Would you rather I called you Margaret? It sounds like your father would prefer that." Jim glanced about the formal living room, almost sorry he had chosen to come. He should have asked a few more questions from the shopkeeper. He was way out of his league.

"My parents have always called me Margaret, but I prefer Maggie. And I think my father likes to scare any boy that comes around. Don't worry about it. I don't. Anyway, I'm glad to see you. Why did you come over?" Maggie cocked her head to the side with an amused look.

"I've been thinking about you for a while. You always seem so nice when you're down at the dock. You have a lovely smile." *That was stupid.* She'd think he was too familiar.

"Well, thank you. I try to be nice, and smiles don't cost a penny. But I guess some of the characters misinterpret them." Maggie shrugged her shoulder and puffed out a sigh. "They get rude sometimes, which makes me angry. But I volunteered to help with that project, so I keep going."

"What project?" Jim cleared his throat and tried to look interested when all he wanted to do was run. He shifted his weight from one side to the other, unable to remain still.

"It's with the Catholic Church. We need more funds for a school gym addition and equipment. The youth group decided to make lunches and sell them. We all take turns, and I have two lunch breaks to cover every second week. We charge a fair price, so there's not much profit, but whatever we make goes back to the church."

"Good plan," Jim commented. He blew out a sigh of anxiety. He wasn't sure what to say next.

"Yes. I think it is." Maggie fiddled with her hands. "Could I get you something to drink? Lemonade, or tea or coffee?"

"No, no thanks." Jim felt as uneasy as Maggie looked. He wondered if he'd made a mistake. "Say, Maggie, are you allowed to date?"

"Sometimes. I'm seventeen now. My father's quite strict, yet if I really want to do something, I usually can." Maggie's eyes danced with mischief, which made Jim dare to hope.

"Could you come out now? We could go to the movies or go for a soft drink?" As Jim waited for her reply, he could feel his face flush.

"I'd love to, but I'm afraid Father won't let me tonight. I could ask him for tomorrow night, though." Her hands continued to fidget in her lap as she smiled encouragingly.

"Sure, that would be great." Jim tapped his thighs nervously, relieved to have made a further commitment but still anxious to get out of there.

"Look, I can't stay. I feel so clumsy that I'm afraid to even talk in here."

"Alright. I'm glad you came." Maggie stood up and walked him to the door, touching his sleeve.

"So am I." Jim's eyes flitted about the hallway before concentrating on her blue eyes. He fingered his hat, glad that she seemed pleased he had come.

"I have to go to the market tomorrow. We need some fresh vegetables. If you're there around 10:00 a.m., I'll let you know if I can go out tomorrow night."

"Good, I'll need to pick some groceries up too, so I'll see you there. Will your mother be with you?"

"Definitely not. My mother's been dead for four years now. It's only my father and me here."

"Sorry to hear that. Both my parents are gone too. It feels strange to be alone."

"So, you can understand then. But I'm getting used to it."

They said their goodbyes, and Jim left, wondering what his chances were. She was becoming almost as special as— Jim pushed the thought away. He was through comparing girls to Lucy. No more. And Maggie was as different from Lucy as possible. Hair, eyes, figure. Nope, Jim thought determinedly. I'm not going to let Lucy's ghost haunt me anymore.

Jim wandered about, killing time before going to Harry's. He decided to visit 'Berto and had a few glasses of homemade wine with him. He took a sip of the dark red wine. The full-bodied tartness of Niagara grapes hid its potency. Jim was careful to nurse the contents as they re-hashed the problems of the loading docks before they left to play poker.

Later, over the noise and smoke of Harry's illicit gaming room, Jim watched unobtrusively as Blacky played five-card stud. Winning a few hands, then losing a few, his mood was as ambivalent as his luck. Frustrated over the last hand, he threw his cards on the table.

"Get me another whiskey," Blacky hollered to Harry.

"Hold yer shirt, Blacky. I'll be right there,"

"Dammit, anyways! I got money here that don' wanna wait, 'n I got a thirst that's only gettin' worse. Bring me a bottle if yer so damn busy, then I can pour my own drinks."

"Bottle costs $5.00 upfront, Blacky."

"Call the cops. That's highway robbery," Blacky complained.

"You want it or not?"

"Yeah. Bring it here." Blacky mumbled.

Jim sauntered up to Blacky and laid his hand on his shoulder. "Hey, Blacky - mind if I sit in?"

"Sure, kid. Hey guys, move over. The kid's goin' to play." A proud smile creased across his lined face as Blacky's eyes lit up with Jim's arrival. He slapped his thighs, then ran his hand over his stubbly chin.

"So, how's your luck tonight?" Jim asked as he handed the deck to shuffle.

"Not bad. The usual, win a few, lose a few." The barkeeper arrived with the Five Star and slapped it on the table. Blacky eyed it hungrily, looked at Jim, then back to the owner. "Ya crazy, Harry? Do ya think I'm gonna buy the whole thing? Take it back and get the kid and I a shot each." Harry stomped back to the bar, muttering angrily as the game continued.

Several hours later, Jim helped his old friend home. His presence had had a positive effect on Blacky, and his game showed it. While Jim lost about $8.00 in the end, Blacky came out twelve ahead, so their finances hadn't suffered.

"It's been a long time, kid." Blacky reminisced as he stumbled over the curb to cross the street.

"Not so long, Blacky." Jim walked close to him, ready to grab him if he stumbled again.

"No, stupid, not the game. I mean, *we've* been *here* a long time." Blacky's voice was slurred but not garbled yet.

"Not even a year, Blacky. That's not long." Jim could see where this was going, but he wanted to avoid this conversation for as long as possible. "Are you sure you're ready to head out, buddy?"

"Soon. Very soon. Are you gonna come with me?"

"I don't know. I'm alright here, and I'm working." Jim shrugged his shoulders. "I went to Maggie's place and saw her tonight."

"Oh ho! So, that's what's holdin' you back?" Blacky teased.

"Maybe. Who knows? Besides, Indian summer's almost over - it's too late to move on."

"Never too late, kid. Never."

The following day was like any other Saturday morning, except there was an odd reticence between them, the first uncomfortable silence they'd ever shared. Jim puttered about trying to ignore the growing tension by tidying their small apartment. Glancing at his watch, he left to meet Maggie and wondered about his friendship with Blacky.

What was going on? In his heart, Jim knew it was coming. Blacky wasn't himself lately. He'd gone from a feisty hobo to a borderline souse and a second or third pick on the docks. Somehow, he'd lost himself here in the big city.

Jim couldn't understand why he let the city life get to him. There seemed no real reason—yet it had. And for Blacky, the only way to regain his pride was to leave. To be free again to move on as the mood took him. Jobs, security —they held no promise for him; they only imprisoned him. Jim would never tie Blacky down or stop him from leaving when the time came. He owed him that much and more. As Jim made his way to Johnson Street to get his weekly groceries, he pushed the dilemma from his mind to concentrate on possibilities.

"Jim?" Maggie's voice caught his attention. They spent a half-hour talking and laughing together as she chose her groceries. In the next three weeks, while Jim grew closer to Maggie, Blacky withdrew. He seldom made a crew anymore.

The effort seemed too great even to attempt it. And when Jim came home, there wasn't much to talk about. Their friendship was strained at best.

"Hey, Blacky, I'm heading out. See you later, ok?" Jim said as he finished the last of their dishes and put the towel away.

"Goin' to Maggie's?"

"Yeah, for a while. Her old man will only let me stay for an hour during the weeknights."

"Why d'ya put up with all that horse shit?" Blacky wondered.

"This is her final year at school before she graduates. It's easier not to rock the boat. Her mother's dead and—"

"Yeah, yeah, who cares? Go on, get outa here."

"Blacky?"

"I mean it, kid. Go. I'm glad for ya, really. Ya found someone ya care for. Great. Y'know, I hate to say it, but I'm ready now, and you're not, and I ain't waitin' anymore." Blacky growled as he slammed his chair back underneath the table. He frowned as he tried to control his temper while a muscle worked at his jawline.

"Look, I'm sorry. I'll stay home tonight, and we'll go play poker."

"Nope, kid, that's it. I've had it with the cards and the booze, and even the money. Look at me—if I don't get outa here, I'm gonna turn into a bum. I was proud to be a travelin' man, but I ain't proud of what I am here. I gotta get that feelin' back, kid. I gotta move on."

"Blacky, look, I'll go with you. Give me a few days to tie things up here. Maggie has to finish the year, and who knows, she may decide to stay longer. I can come back for her later."

"No, kid - yer not gonna lose another one. Face it. You

and I are cut from a different cloth. We were good together for a while, but things change." Blacky avoided Jim's eyes and took a deep breath, exhaling slowly. "It's time."

"C'mon Blacky," Jim wheedled, trying to hold back the inevitable.

Blacky lifted his shoulders and straightened. His dark eyes held Jim's. "Don't push it, kid. Let it go. We'll run into each other again one day. We each got something we gotta do, and if this girl's right for ya, then that's the end of yer travelin' days." Blacky headed to the chipped plywood dresser and threw some clothing in a bag.

"Blacky, I'm going to miss you."

"Shut up, kid."

Jim walked with him across the river, down to the main rail depot. It was a clear, starlit night, and soon they began teasing each other, remembering countless other nights they had walked together. The familiar noises of the rail yard soon caught their ear as Jim saw the first genuine smile cross Blacky's face in a long while. He caught the glint of adventure in his friend's eyes again and realized Blacky had made the right decision for himself.

Blacky *was* a traveling man. They shook hands and slapped each other's shoulders. Finally, with a mutual mock salute, they went their separate ways, thankful that their sadness was gentled by good memories and an acceptance of another time gone by.

～

JIM CURSED AND SWORE. He swung out at every bush and kicked every rock in his path. It was no use. If only he had known the future! He would have gone with Blacky had he known the extent of Mr. Browning's determination. A convent—so *Margaret* could concentrate on her studies, her father had advised stiffly. *Bull shit*, Jim had replied boldly. *You sent her away from me.* Her father had only glared at him, turned his nose up, then closed the door.

He should have known something like that would have happened. Although they hadn't been intimate, they had learned a lot about each other in a short time. He was sure Maggie was starting to care a lot for him. Her father must have sensed their deepening relationship. He wondered if she left dutifully or if she'd fought against it. Couldn't she have left a message somewhere? Damn.

Jim went into Harry's place and proceeded to get drunk, ordering shots of whiskey with a beer chaser. He shunned the advances of several of his fellow stevedores to talk or play cards. Harry watched him surreptitiously until he finally guided Jim to a storage room and sat him down, propped him against the wall to sleep it off. Safer in there, Harry knew, than dead drunk in the street.

Surprised, Harry watched Jim follow the same pattern again the following day and the day after. Jim hardly spoke, only occasionally cursing, which was so out of character that Harry finally gave him a heart-to-heart, which he seldom gave. He figured he had enough of his own problems, and a souse didn't want anyone's advice. But the kid was lost without Blacky.

"Gimme another shot, Harry." A bleary-eyed, bewhiskered bum whispered.

"Gotta headache, Jim?"

"Nothing a shot won't fix." Jim couldn't meet the bartender's eyes. He rubbed a hand over his stubbled face, then through his hair as he began mumbling to himself.

"You knucklehead—you've been on a bender for the better part of three days. I ain't keeping you here again. If you get falling down drunk again today, I'm gonna kick your worthless ass out of here."

"Take a powder, Harry. Give me a goddam drink."

Jim's unfocused eyes and slurred speech confirmed Harry's decision. "Bar's closed to you, Jim. Go home and sleep it off. You've flipped your lid, and I don't know what the hell to do with you."

"Nothing's wrong with me." Jim hiccupped, then wiped his hand across his mouth. At one time, he would've been embarrassed with himself, but right now, he didn't care. "Quit being a buzz killer and pour me another shot of whiskey. Maybe my luck will change."

"Oh, quit feeling sorry for yourself. Never thought you were a quitter, a schnook like the rest of the drunks around here." Harry wiped the bar down and ignored Jim's request for another drink.

"Quit busting my chops-I'm not a sch-schnook." Jim sputtered indignantly.

"Sure 'n hell looks like it." Harry undid his apron and called one of his waitresses to come and take over. "I don't do this very often, kid, but I'm taking you home."

"Go to hell, leave me alone," Jim mumbled defensively. Yet, he had no strength left to fight Harry's firm grip. It was a short three blocks to his apartment, but Jim felt like it took hours to get there. Once inside, Harry laid him on a cot, looked around, found him a puke bucket, and left.

It took Jim two full days to recuperate. He was disgusted when he eventually took stock of his vomit-covered clothes and red squinting eyes. He showered and shaved, then forced himself to eat. Looking around his apartment, Jim thought about his future. He grabbed his jacket and went outside into the chilly November morning.

Jim walked around the familiar neighborhoods, then

down onto the piers. The sky was a blanket of grey, while a slight wind on the lake made whitecaps form on the charcoal water. Three huge ships were in, and the sounds of machinery and men working enveloped him. Usually, the sounds and the smell of the docking yards pleased him, and he'd generally liked working there.

Today, there was nothing. And Jim finally understood how Blacky must have felt. Now he knew he couldn't have waited either. It was time for him to move on, although this trip would be his first alone on the lines.

CHAPTER 8

Smash! Bellows of pain and curses of anger floated through the third-story bedroom window. Though the room was still warm and muggy, Jim closed it, shutting away the sounds of another Friday night drunken brawl in Noranda, Quebec. He finished buttoning his pants, walked to the coffee table, and poured himself a whiskey.

"Why don't you leave it open, sweetie? It's so hot in here," complained Penny. Jim eyed the buxom blonde sitting in her slip at her boudoir, combing her thick dark hair, trying vainly to create kiss curls at her cheeks. "Damn heat. I can't do anything with my hair." She banged the brush down on the mahogany surface, then caught the look of displeasure on Jim's face in the round mirror. She slid across the stool and approached him.

"Oh well, it'll only get mussed up again soon, won't it?" She moved closer to him, her firm breasts jiggling slightly, enticing him to look at her. She reached out and put her hand against his chest, splaying her fingers in his coarse, curly hair. Her blue eyes had a longing that he thought he had recently satisfied.

"Not tonight, doll. I've got a meeting. I'll call you in a couple of days, alright?" Jim kissed her lightly, pretending not to see the disappointment. He grabbed his shirt from the chair and slipped it on, buttoning it quickly.

"I'll be here unless Rejeanne comes over. Then who knows where we'll end up." Penny moved aside quickly and searched among her toiletries for her cigarette case.

"Look, I warned you I wouldn't be able to stay long."

"I know, I know. Go ahead. I'm not stopping you. I'll probably go to the movies. At least it's cool in there. So, go!" Penny waved her hand towards the door, but her forced vitality didn't go unnoticed, and neither did her trembling hands.

"Look, Penny—we've been through this before. Why don't you let me go? Find yourself some nice guy who'll look after you?"

"No. No way. Hey, look, don't worry about it. I've thought a lot about us, and I've decided to wait for you. One of these days, I'll be more important to you than some damn union. Besides," she joked, "There aren't too many other men around these days - the war's got them all. Whoops, sorry—I didn't mean anything by that." Penny groaned and slid her eyes to the window. She'd hit a sore spot. "Look, honey, I know this union's important to you, but please be careful. If the bosses ever get wind you're trying to organize a strike, I'm going to find you dead on the street somewhere."

"Now it's your turn, not to worry. I learned plenty of tricks when I hopped the trains. I know the ropes. I'll be ok."

"Good." Suddenly Penny's blue eyes brightened again. "I hope you get a good turnout tonight. Say, why don't we kick up our heels tomorrow night? The Moose community hall's having a fundraiser for war bonds. Those foreigners sure know how to throw a party, and I'm just dying to go. We'll have a gas. Please?"

Jim laughed at her coquettish wiles and drew her to him, squeezing her curvaceous body close to his.

"Alright, alright, we'll go," Jim replied. Penny kissed him soundly and pressed her body close to him again, offering more. Jim pushed her aside gently, smacking her derriere lightly. "I gotta go, Penn. I'll call you in a few days." He dropped a deuce on the dresser. "Get yourself a new dress for the dance, ok?" Without waiting for an answer, Jim grabbed his hat and slung his jacket over his shoulder.

Penny swallowed hard and smiled back at him. She hated it when he did that, but she shrugged her shoulders to feign indifference. "Bye. Don't be a stranger—you don't have to wait until Saturday night to come over. We can grab some lunch or something."

Jim smiled, gave her the thumbs-up sign, and then closed the door gently behind him. With union business now occupying his mind, he went bounding down the two steep flights of stairs with Penny already gone from his mind. He side-stepped the rowdy people in the street, oblivious to the sights and sounds of the run-down neighborhood. People were sitting out on their porches or steps, looking for relief from the humid summer night. It wasn't unusual for a brawl or two to break out on a Saturday night as patrons left the beer parlor a few blocks away. Tonight wasn't any different. It was a hard town, a tough town, yet Jim had visions for it.

Jim reviewed his situation since he arrived three years ago. Even though his finances had improved dramatically, he was still boarding in the same house he had moved into. Giving up liquor and speakeasies, Jim was determined to carve out a future for himself and saved every cent he could.

When Jim arrived in the spring of '41, the mines in Rouyn and Noranda were expanding. He found work processing the valuable iron, copper ore, and other metals used in growing car manufacturing facilities. However, when conscription came, the Rouyn mineral company he worked for proclaimed him invaluable to the war effort, so he was exempted from the draft. The army patrol often examined the creased paper in his wallet, looking for eligible men trying to elude enlistment.

He should feel fortunate that he was safe and working for the war effort, but it always made him uncomfortable that he was safe here in Canada rather than going into battle. Jim knew this union business only assuaged the guilty feelings he harbored because he was excused from recruitment. He needed to feel his efforts were almost as important as the men who had gone to war.

After listening to the DPs working within the mines, Jim found a cause he could get behind. These *displaced persons* who'd come before the war exploded in central and eastern European countries were eager to start a new life here. They explained the labor systems they worked under back home, surprised that it wasn't a universal benefit in a progressive country like Canada. Those skilled tradesmen and laborers encouraged Jim to join their cause to create a better standard of life.

In his mind, both were fighting for justice. Now, Jim was entrenched in the secrecy of creating a labor union for better safety precautions and wages. Tonight had the potential to change a lot of minds. To give them the courage to force their employers to listen to their demands.

Jim felt the adrenaline build as he took the necessary precautions to avoid detection. He took a circuitous route to the basement at the Moose Hall, often backtracking and checking his trail. At twenty-three, Jim had the experience and a keen sixth sense for the unexpected. Tonight, he had to be extra careful. He didn't want any unwelcome surprises for their guest speaker.

Michael Latimer!

At long last, he had convinced a union organizer to come and speak to his fellow laborers. Michael would be there to advise them and help them make their guild effective. His speeches were energizing and focused on obtaining results. A Red or a Communist, that's what some called Latimer, but Jim didn't care what he was. As long as the organizer could give them the direction and the tools to establish a strong union.

Power! Leadership!

That's what they needed. And Jim craved it. He craved the security it offered. Because never again did he want to go through those lonely, wandering years. Those wasted years. He needed to be part of something big.

Jim's thoughts focused on the agenda for tonight. He'd advocated a strike for some time now, but everyone was afraid. The Polish, Ukrainians, Germans, and Finns, otherwise known as the *Fros*, the shortened version of foreigner, were angling for an eight-hour workday. The locals had listened to their tales of the benefits of having a union, but they weren't convinced it would work in Canada. Maybe that would change tonight.

Jim glanced about him and slowed his pace. He knelt on one knee, pretended to tie his shoelace, and listened intently for slowing footsteps. Satisfied he was alone, he stood up, retraced the last block, and turned into the alley. Four houses down on the left, Jim hopped a picket fence and approached the basement door. A match lit up, illuminating the smoker's face.

"Blacky!" Jim's jaw dropped in surprise as he saw his old friend keeping watch. "Well, I'll be damned, good to see you."

"Jim, ya son of a bitch!" Blacky reached out and pumped his hand vigorously. "Should'a known it was someone like you getting this thing goin'. How ya been?"

"Good, good. I didn't know you were traveling with Michael Latimer. Since when?"

"Oh, it must be a couple of years now. I heard him yapping at one of the camps outside Windsor, and he made a lotta sense to me. He needed some... protection, so I volunteered. There's a lotta big shots out there that don' like him. His work's kinda dangerous to his health." Blacky shrugged a shoulder as he took another drag from his cigarette. "It suits me fine—we're always on the move, and I feel like I'm part of somethin' important. Too old to go to war, so I'm doing what I can. What are ya up to? All settled down and married 'n all?" Blacky's heavy-lidded eyes scanned his old friend.

"Settled, I guess, but not married." Jim shrugged nonchalantly.

"That broad you were lovesick over, what happened?"

"Who knows? It's all history now anyway. Besides, I'm too busy now to be any good to a wife." Jim slapped Blacky on the shoulder, grinning with the joy of seeing him again.

"Ain't that the God's truth. Organizin' and workin' don' leave much time left over. At least yer here and not over *there* fighting. I guess yer exempt?"

"Yeah. Somebody has to make the ammunition and metal to fight them." Jim's indecision showed on his face. "I tried to fight the exemption but lost."

"S'alright, kid, you're doing your bit here. And this can get bloody dangerous too. Most places are goin' with the movement, but I've seen some guys beat up bad, almost crippled over this thing. What's the story 'round here? The company gonna give up easy?"

"So far, so good. The company's not really making any trouble, but they're not taking us seriously either. They're trying to keep the fros from socializing with the locals to avoid any discussions of the unions they had back in their homeland. We're not allowed to talk union at all at work. When we bring up a gripe, all they ever say is that they'll look into it."

"And nothin' gets done, right?" Blacky shook his head with frustration.

"Right." Jim nodded discouragingly.

"But they're sure making lots of goddam money over this bloody war. To hear them talk, their war effort's outa the goodness of their heart."

"You got that right. And I heard through the grapevine the company recently acquired another government contract. The big push is on to produce more. They can't hire a graveyard shift, not enough skilled labor, so they'll push our hours longer."

"You guys get overtime?"

"Huh," Jim grunted. "I only wish."

"What's the town like? Does the company sponsor housing, a hospital, or anything else for their workers?"

"There's a Catholic hospital here, run by the sisters. They do their best with the modest equipment they have. Anything serious has to go to Montreal, but that's at least three hours from here. The wages aren't high enough for most people to buy a home, which creates a problem with housing. They have good company rentals for management, but the family rental units aren't great."

"Listen to Michael tonight, kid. Those are all things ya'll

be able to negotiate for. Wages are only part of the answer. Bargaining for employee benefits will make a huge difference around here."

Another man sidled by them into the basement, and Jim checked his pocket watch. "Go on inside," Blacky advised. "I'll be the last one in."

Jim nodded and stepped inside the low-hung door, stooping slightly. Inside, rows of planks mounted on bricks filled the room. A thick haze of cigarette smoke settled around the murmuring crowd of men. He made his way towards the front, where a rough dais stood. Sitting behind it, shuffling through some papers, was the man Jim had contacted.

"Mr. Latimer?"

"Yessir, in the flesh. What can I do for you?"

"I'm Jim Taylor. Guess you could call me the chief steward for this area."

"Nice to meet you." Latimer shook Jim's hand briskly. "I hear you're having problems getting the men and the company to listen to you?"

"Yeah. I mean, the men want things to be different, but that's all they're willing to do. Right now, all I hear is them complaining and wishing it would happen."

"Well, you can't blame them, son. Most of the fellas workin' here are older, and they've all seen the soup kitchens, the railways, and the dole. They're used to a bum rap. They have steady work now, so they don't want to rock the boat."

"Yes, I know. I was one of them. I used to run with Blacky."

"Aha. Good man, Blacky. Wily as a fox, I suppose that's why he's still around."

"Yeah. He's tough, and he's smart. I probably wouldn't

have made it without him. Figures Blacky would turn up with you. I don't think he'll ever settle down." Jim shrugged. "It's been a few years since I've seen him. I'm glad he's traveling with you. He's a guy you can count on."

"He's as loyal as they come." Michael agreed. "Some folks never settle down, and he's probably one of them. That's what the depression of the '30s did to them. To others, like the men here, it made them fearful. Afraid to stand up for themselves." Michael's voice grew louder with conviction as he shook a forefinger at Jim. "But *that's* the point. To never be powerless again. A united force has the clout to make even governments listen. You'll see."

The basement door closed loudly, and Blacky let out a loud whistle to quieten the men. Jim took his place at the dais and began. "This is our tenth monthly meeting. Tonight, we have a special guest speaker. But before I give him the stand, I've got a few things to report: The recommendation we made on safety rails on the stack have been rejected. The comment was, we should use more common sense."

The men laughed at that remark, some noting how fast they'd be fired if they refused to climb up the eighty-foot chimney stack on a windy day.

"And you probably heard, Dave Johnson died from internal bleeding after the accident he had in his forklift. His family will have to move out of the company duplex. We'll pass the hat around later." Jim cleared his throat. "We're also having trouble collecting some of the dues. I need help. I can't manage all the collecting alone. Any volunteers?"

Jim collected union dues in person each month, but he was often avoided. It wasn't a pleasant job, and now Jim needed help. He couldn't work his job and handle all the worker's complaints too. He doubted he'd get assistance, but he'd ask again. When an older man tipped his hat, Jim sighed a breath of relief. "Thanks, Mr. Tierney. I'll talk to you later." Jim eyed the crowd through a haze of cigarette smoke, his pulse quickening. "Now, I'd like to introduce our union rep for Quebec – Mr. Michael Latimer. Please give him your attention."

Latimer stood up amid a wave of subdued applause.

"Thank you. I'm glad to be here. I understand your local has been organized for almost a year now. And some of you are wondering why you're paying union dues every month, and nothing is changing. Right?"

Mumbles of agreement accompanied the nodding heads. "You've all been Mr. Nice Guys. Right? Minding your business, following the manual for registering complaints. And has it gotten you anywhere?"

"No! The company never does anything." shouted one of the auxiliary stewards. "And there's not enough men who wanna help us get more support for a strike. My wife's getting darn sick of it. So far, all this union's done is make more work for me." A few other men clapped lightly, supporting his stand.

"That's always a concern at the beginning. But don't give up. When's the last time there was a raise here?" Latimer asked as he strode across the stage with his arms spread out, looking for an answer.

Jim spoke up. "About a year and a half ago, some men were given a two cents an hour raise - but not everyone got it."

"And I've heard the company will be reporting a healthy year-end report to its shareholders in September. So, what are you guys waiting for? What better time to strike for higher wages?"

Mr. Thompson stood up, nervously fingering his cap. "There's a war going on. I don't want people thinking we're trying to get rich on the back of our soldiers overseas."

"The company will be using exactly that against you. You need to send a different message. You must force them to acknowledge your value in helping them mine and process the metals needed for the war effort. The work *you* do *is* dangerous. You are working without a contract. Where's the justice in that? A healthy working relationship means give and take on both sides. It's not a recipe for the rich to get richer on the backs of cheap labor. Remember that."

The men looked at each other uncertainly, yet a tremor of excitement rippled the room. With each challenge presented came encouragement which gave the men confidence. The meeting that started with discouragement was now optimistic that a better future wasn't far away. When Latimer stepped down, Jim viewed the crowd that was no longer frightened but united and strong.

As he smiled and shook hands with his fellow workers, Jim hoped they'd stay strong. For better or for worse, they were on their way.

"MAY HE REST IN PEACE, in the Glory of the Lord." Father Antonio made the sign of the cross over the casket and then returned to the dais. The smell of incense permeated the church as the congregation supported each other in their grief.

"Amen." The deep voice of almost two hundred men and their families echoed the sadness felt there today.

"Jim, would you like to say a few words?" Father Antonio

asked. Jim stepped forward with his hands folded in front of him. He looked around at his men and took a deep breath, wondering how he could do homage to a fallen hero. Blacky had been his hero for more years than he cared to admit. This violent turn in the strike visibly shook some, and fear showed on their face. Others looked defiant and angry. They had all lost a brother to the cause.

Jim cleared his throat, and his first words were shaky and low. "Blacky was an inspiration to most of you who got to know him." As he searched the faces of the men he had stood and worked alongside, he gathered strength in their trust. They were looking up to him, following him. He straightened his back and raised his voice to address the entire congregation.

"Blacky worked hard for the union. When Mr. Latimer left us, Blacky stayed behind to help with this strike. He taught us by example to be strong and stand together for our beliefs. I've known Blacky for almost seven years. He was my closest friend and a great motivator for many. I let him down once, yet he never thought less of me. He knew the human spirit and accepted it. He went on with his life, staying true to his own set of values."

"And what I know for sure is this: If any of you let this— this accident divide the union, he'll come back and haunt you. His death was *not* in vain. He *died* defending our picket lines while helping us accomplish our goal. The scabs never came through." Jim paused as a smattering of applause rippled through the church. "The cops backed off, and so did the company. A settlement's near." Jim fingered the cuffs on his suit's sleeve, trying to control his trembling voice.

"I respected and cared for Blacky. As did many people. He never asked for it, but he earned it with the high regard he gave to everyone he met. He always looked you in the eye, and his word was as good as gold. Our union will dedicate this day in memoriam, so his courage for our men will never be forgotten." Jim stepped down and walked by the casket, reverently stopping to put his hand on it.

"Amen." The priest returned to the dais advising the men to join him at the church hall afterward for a wake. Jim stayed awhile, then left to finalize negotiations with their employer, his wooden features showing no sign of emotion. The crowd of men stayed all afternoon, sharing memories. Sympathetic wives brought in sandwiches at dinner as the men sat and waited.

They were reluctant to leave, sensing something was in the air. And finally, at about 8:30, Jim walked back in. He strode to the front of the hall. The men had fallen silent at his arrival. There was no need to shout.

"Men! Thanks to you and Blacky, the company has agreed to a four percent raise. Congratulations." Jim offered a small smile, but the victory had come at a steep price.

"About damned time," yelled some of the men as they turned to shake one another's hand.

"They have also agreed to supply $3,000.00 worth of equipment to St. Joseph's hospital. We'll finally have a decent hospital."

This time a round of applause went up. In so many accidents similar to Blacky's, time was of the essence. Transporting an injured patient to the big city often cost them their lives.

"That one was for Blacky," murmured one of the men.

"This one was for ALL of us," Jim replied, tears filling his eyes. He circulated in the room, shaking hands and rubbing the shoulders of the men who had finally united.

CHAPTER 9

Jim leaned against a post outside the Windsor railway station, watching another trainload of GI's passing through. Some were on crutches or sporting a sling, all more slender and serious than when they left their homeland. Some disembarked to waiting arms, and others traveled onward to the west. The war was over. Their war and his battle.

Jim's title as the chief steward had thrown him into conflict many times in the last three years. He remembered the strike of '42 that lasted one and a half weeks. They had stood up against an armed police squad sent by the company to break the picket lines so that scabs could enter. Blacky had died, and all for three cents an hour, a four percent raise.

Over the years, Jim's calm demeanor had often quietened the restless bickering of men fearful of their future. And after Blacky's death, he began carrying a loaded gun to protect those around him or diffuse a situation that reason couldn't penetrate. The affair with Penny had died some time ago, much to his relief. Thankfully, Jim had no one he needed to account to or hold him back. He could dedicate his life to a cause that had claimed his friend.

They said Jim had guts, and from his strength came respect and, later, power. Families in trouble called him, so he used his position to help resolve their difficulties. Whether it was health or finances, he lent an ear and then compassionately set the wheels in motion for his union brothers to get the help they needed. And in return, these people gave him what they could—a life of Sunday dinners, companionship, and confidential reports.

At first, Jim resisted. But he soon realized how often these tips ended up benefiting the union. So, he listened, and sometimes he acted. When Jim received a tip on the assay of the latest drilled core in the nearby Kekeko Hills, he wrestled with his conscience. And in the end, he decided to take a personal risk. In an impulsive gesture, he invested heavily in Silver Arrow, who ironically drilled into a vein of high-quality gold. Jim's original investment of four hundred dollars into shares that he bought at twenty-one cents each skyrocketed. He sold half his investment within six months when it reached six dollars a share. Last week Jim sold the balance at nine dollars a share.

Ever since Jim took the plunge into the stock market, he'd felt his old yearnings re-surface. He'd accomplished everything he had set out to do, establishing a unionized workforce. With a healthy bank account, it was time to move on. Sitting on the wooden bench waiting for the eleven a.m. passenger train, he experienced the almost forgotten thrill of adventure. And with a spiffy new double-breasted suit, two leather suitcases, and a positive attitude, he looked forward to a new horizon. The winds of change had caught him again, calling and inviting him to explore—this time with money in his pocket.

Yet before he could head west to the Pacific Ocean, to the land of milk and honey in British Columbia, he had some long-standing problems to solve. Jim glanced at his ticket to Prince Albert and sighed. He had known in his heart for years that Lucy had abandoned him. He needed to find out why she hadn't written and what had happened to her. Without facing the truth, Jim knew she would forever haunt him. He'd never make another woman happy if he couldn't push Lucy out of his mind completely. Jim hadn't seen her since the summer of '37 - almost eight years ago. Time didn't stop her face from appearing in his dreams or stop the semi-conscious drive to find a woman that would obliterate her memory.

Maggie might've been able to do it, but since even that spark hadn't been allowed to flare, he had resisted baring his heart for another woman. He had to go back and face Lucy to push aside her haunting tiger eyes. Only answers and reality would do that.

"Got a light?"

"Sure." Jim dug a match from the box in his suit pocket, struck it against the bench, and politely offered it to the young man. Snapping back to the present, he was pleased to find the young man seated next to him, his duffel bag at his feet.

"Army or Navy?" Jim asked.

"Army. How could you tell?"

"Buzz cut." Jim pointed to his hair. "You're not in uniform, but that gives it away. On your way home or going somewhere?"

"I'm heading out. I've been home a week, and I can't take it. I'm going to find something new."

"I thought you'd be glad to be home." Jim eyed him carefully, trying to figure out what his story was.

"Yeah, well - things change." The sailor took another deep drag of his cigarette, then blew O's in the air. "I'm Keith. Keith Hansen." He offered his handshake.

"Nice to meet you, Keith. I'm Jim Taylor."

"Where were you stationed, Jim?"

"I wasn't. I was needed for the war effort, processing metal at Rouyn-Noranda. Never felt right about it but couldn't get out of it either."

"Yeah. I can understand that. Well, you did your job, and I did mine." Keith took another deep drag from his cigarette, then butted it out on the sidewalk. "My folks want me to work at their hardware and tackle store now. My girlfriend was one of the nice ones - she waited for me." Confusion crept into his voice. "But I can't. I just *can't* walk back into that life."

"I can understand that. The war changed everything. Give them time. They'll probably adjust, and so will you." Jim said.

"Nope. We're already arguing. I can't take up where I left off, letting my parents and Vivian call the shots. They think I'm still the same kid that left four years ago. I'm not ready to be told what to do again. Besides, they probably wouldn't like the new me."

Jim nodded in sympathy. "Helluva problem, isn't it? It doesn't sound like you're ready to settle down. You probably don't even know which way to turn." Jim laid a hand on his shoulder. "It must be tough, but you're probably doing the right thing. Did you let them know you were leaving?"

Keith nodded. "I told my mom this morning - after Dad left for work. I didn't want to leave angry. And if I'd have told my dad, there would've been arguments. Kind of chicken shit, I know, but Mom's great - she'll smooth it out. I told her I'd be back."

Jim smiled remembering his parting promise to Lucy. "Sure, you will. I'm going to Prince Albert for a while and then heading to B.C. If you want to join me, you're welcome."

"Great. I wasn't sure where I'd go, but I knew it would be either the Maritimes or B.C. I've always loved the ocean. Most of my family have made fishing their livelihood. Although right now, the farther away I am, the less likely I'll be talked into returning."

The announcer called Jim's train, and Keith scurried to the wicket, purchasing his ticket to join him. The two of them boarded the train, laughing. Each had lived very different lives, but for a moment, they looked like ordinary young men, excited and anxious to embrace a new future.

As Jim watched the countryside slip away, one window frame at a time, his thoughts drifted back. It seemed a lifetime ago that Jim had traveled the rail lines, never knowing where his next meal would be, swallowing his pride and surviving the private shame the depression caused him.

"Did you ever hop the trains, Keith?"

"No, never did. I was lucky. Our family fished and ran a hardware store, so we held things together even when times were tough. I was the first in my family to graduate, and soon after, I enlisted in the Army. What about you?"

"My mother died when I was twelve, and my pa was a fur trapper. When I was seventeen, I went with him on his last run to the Churchill River Basin. He died up there, and long story short, I found myself alone, broke, and looking for work. Like so many others, that meant riding the rails."

"I can't imagine doing that so young. That must have been dangerous."

"I was lucky. I met an older hobo who went by the name of Blacky. He showed me the ropes. We traveled together for a few years." Jim recounted his trapping and hobo life, often inserting humor to make light of his journey. As Jim shared his stories, he felt the pain and despair of those years begin to disappear. And it felt good. It was ok. He survived.

Jim shared his troubled times and recent successes with a newfound friend at his side, then listened, sometimes enviously, while Keith described some of his wartime experiences. He was sure that Keith omitted the worst of them. He focused only on the triumphant battles and the glorious reception as they liberated Holland, Belgium, and France. True, Keith's life in the army had been much more dangerous and different from Jim's, but they both experienced fear and faced the challenges before them. The conductor admonished them to be quiet as midnight fell, so they searched for an empty row of seats to stretch out and rest. The rolling motion of the train lulled them to sleep.

"Wake up, lazybones! Let's go get some joe."

Jim rolled over, opening his eyes reluctantly. "You're not in the army anymore - why don't you sleep in?"

"Hell, I have slept in. I'd have been up for a couple of hours at least. Come on, Jim – let's get cracking." Keith looked even younger and more wholesome than before.

Jim checked his watch. 5:45. With a groan, he got up, stretched, and found the washroom. After a wash and shave, he felt almost human again and joined Keith in the diner for breakfast.

"So, what's so important in Prince Albert?" Keith inquired.

"Not much in Prince Albert. I have a few things to check out in Big River - a small farming community a few hours northwest of it."

"Unfinished business?" Keith's eyebrows arched, indicating he'd like to hear more.

"Yeah - you could say that," Jim replied. "Oh, what the hell - you know half my life now anyway. I left a girl behind in '38. I wrote to her every chance I had, yet she never answered me." Jim spread his hands, questioning the reason. "I've never understood. We were young, but I know she loved me. She said she'd follow when I got settled, but it never happened." Jim shrugged and shook his head. "I tried to forget her and put it all behind me, but I've never been able to. I need to understand why she never stayed in touch."

"You can't go back to the way it was, Jim. I found that out. You're right, though. Until I went home, I thought I'd be able to step back into my old life, and everything would be the same."

"I know. My girlfriend probably won't even remember me," Jim covered up his apprehension that this would be an emotional disaster. "I'm not sure what I feel for her is real anymore. Before I go west, I want to iron it out."

"I think I'll wait in Prince Albert for you. Check out the place and leave you alone for a while."

"It shouldn't take long - I could be back within a day or two. She's probably happily married by now. I'll send you a telegraph if there's anything promising left there."

"Sure. And you can leave your stuff with me if you want and come back when you're ready. I'm not on any schedule anymore. I'm in no rush to move on. You never know what could happen there or what I'll find in P.A." Keith shrugged as if he didn't have a care in the world and lit another cigarette.

By now, the train had left Ontario, passing through the Manitoba countryside. The landscape of rolling foothills and numerous small lakes and estuaries reminded Jim of his early days with his dad, then his time with Blacky. He grew increasingly silent as his mind and heart slipped backward in time. Keith, attuned to his mood, played games of solitaire while keeping an eye out for attractive girls.

October in Manitoba was a glorious month. The air was crisp and cold, the skies a bright blue. The forests were mainly coniferous compared to the evergreens in Ontario, creating a landscape alive with color. Bright flashes of red and gold mixed with the russet and the evergreen colored the countryside. Gradually, the scenic beauty melted Jim's apprehension, and he put his impending rendezvous in perspective. They reached Winnipeg and switched trains, his mood noticeably lighter and more carefree. And when Keith struck up a conversation with two young ladies in their section, Jim joined in. The afternoon and evening flew by until the ladies retreated to their sleeper section, and the guys searched for a comfortable place to stretch out and catch some sleep.

The following day, Jim rose early and watched the endless plains of Saskatchewan roll by. Only the occasional flock of Canada Geese feeding on the leftover grain in the fields gave life to the landscape of stubby farm sections lying dormant. The sky was an overcast grey, a melancholy acceptance of winter coming. It matched Jim's mood as he sat staring out the window, wondering if his decision had been wise.

"Definitely not," Jim murmured aloud.

"My, my. Talking to yourself—that could be dangerous." Keith teased as he plunked into the seat beside him. "What's the matter with you this morning? You look grumpy."

"Nothing." Jim drummed his fingernails on the armrest while his foot bounced a mile a minute as he tried to diffuse the nervous energy he was feeling.

"Worried about meeting her?" Keith cocked his head to the side, his eyebrows lifting.

Jim shrugged. "What's there to be worried about? I don't even know why I'm going there. What we had's gone. Maybe we should buy our tickets in Prince Albert and head straight to Vancouver. What do you think?'

"Sorry, buddy. You can't take the easy way out. You have to get her out of your mind, see for yourself what she's done with her life. You'll never get over her if you don't know what happened. You'll always wonder."

"I don't know." Jim breathed a sigh of frustration and then ran his hand over his face.

"C'mon, Jim. You're almost there. Get it over with. You can do this, and then we'll head out." Keith punched him lightly on the shoulder.

"Yeah. I guess so." Jim observed the outskirts of Prince Albert. "Won't be long that we'll be at the station, then we'll figure out how to handle this."

"OK. I'll be back in a few minutes. I need to have at least one more cup of joe." When Keith returned, he had the same two girls with him. They gave him their phone numbers hesitantly amid blushes and laughter. Keith retrieved their suitcases from the overhead compartment as the train slowed and jerked to a stop. Jim, more nervous than he could admit, watched as the girls fell captive to his friend's irresistible magic. They waved goodbye and blew kisses to him as they reminded him to call. Jim guessed that Keith probably had a lot of time to make up for, and with his dazzling charm, he'd be breaking a few hearts.

Making their way along the crowded station platform, they looked for an available taxi. "You sure were a dead-beat." Keith teased as he strode confidently alongside Jim, eyeing every skirt around them.

"I don't think the girls even noticed. Besides, I don't care if they did. You were handling both of them fine."

"How can you tell I love women?" Keith laughed. "I don't even have to lay them. I really love being around them, watching them primp for me and flirt."

"Yeah, sure." Jim watched the twinkle in his friend's eyes and the bouncy step in his walk.

Keith was in high spirits and winked at his new friend. "Well—I don't say no to them, that's for sure. But it's the game that counts."

Jim laughed at his buddy's enthusiasm. "We better get you your own room quick, or the first thing you know, you'll be shot in the ass by some jealous husband."

"That's not going to happen. I'm not crazy—there are lots of gals around. I don't need to borrow any."

"Taxi!" They both yelled simultaneously. Running, they caught a cab and left the noise of the station.

JIM LEFT the Arlington Hotel the following morning with a strange feeling in his chest. Part of him was hopeful, yet a part dreaded the knowledge he felt compelled to find. He went to a cafe and ordered a hearty breakfast of bacon and eggs with hash browned potatoes. Jim drank several cups of coffee while reading the local paper, trying to catch the names of people he might know. The want ad section cried for construction laborers, so he filed the information for later reference. Jim had helped many families in work bees and had a general knowledge of framing homes. Pushing his coffee cup aside finally, he confronted his most imminent problem.

Lucy. He couldn't face anything else until he saw her.

Keith agreed to stick around the area for a month while Jim tackled his past. He'd leave a forwarding address at the

Arli if he moved on. Keith would find some temporary work and look the area over. After making several inquiries, Jim eventually bargained to rent an older model truck from a Ford dealership for a week. Leaving a hefty fifty-dollar deposit, he headed Northwest over the Saskatchewan River towards home.

Home. Nostalgia washed over him. He needed to see the Madsens again, the family he had grown up with. He let his thoughts wander and thought of Larry and Brian, his childhood friends. Even if the thing with Lucy didn't work out, he wanted to see them again. If they were still there, of course. They could have enlisted and made another life for themselves as he had. He doubted he'd ever return after this trip.

Jim took his time traveling the gravel country roads, spotting landmarks. Memories had softened, and he smiled as he thought of his naïve outlook on life at seventeen. Occasionally, he heard a far-away hoot of passing rail cars, triggering a memory of his first meeting with Blacky. So many hard times, yet so many good times too. Thankfully, time had done its magic and had dulled the more painful emotions. The only wound that hadn't healed was Lucy. But he was going to fix that, once and for all.

Far ahead, he recognized the granary. He scanned the area for Matthew's two-story home. All that remained was a stone chimney, as the old place had probably burned to the ground years ago. His heart sank as he wondered how many people would never be in his life again. About a half-mile over to the right of it was a newer, one-level home. Jim turned into the laneway, hoping he would know the occupants.

An older woman came out of the house, craning to see who had approached. Her grey hair was laced with white and pulled back from her creased face. She wiped her hands on her printed apron and warily descended the steps.

"Can I help ya, son?" her shaky voice enquired. "Ya lost 'er somethin'?"

"I was looking for Matthew Spencer. He and his family used to live in that house back there," he pointed to the crumbling rock formation.

"I'm Matthew's wife. He's been dead two years now. I don't 'member meeting ya before," she eyed him suspiciously now.

"I'm sorry about Matthew, ma'am." Jim took off his hat. "I worked with him for part of a summer close to seven years ago. When I left town, I gave him my horse."

"Oh, you're the one? I 'member Matt talkin' 'bout you." Again, a suspicious look crossed her face. "Ya want yer horse back? He's just an old thing now, sway back 'n all."

"No, no. I don't want the horse."

"He sired three colts, all good horses now. Ya want one of 'em?"

"No, I don't need one. They're your horses. I only wanted to catch up on the news and see some people."

"In that case, c'mon in - what I cain't tell ya ain't worth knowin'. All my kids 'cept one's married and spread out around these parts. When they come home, I hear all the gossip," she chuckled. "Can I get ya some coffee?"

"Yes, ma'am," Jim said.

"Look at my new house." Mrs. Spencer waved at the shingled home with pride. "We were only five of us left, livin' in that old house, when my boy left a bucket of cleaning rags near the stove. The fire nearly killed us, and when help came, it was too late. My oldest kids gathered a work party with the church not long after, and everybody pitched in and built us this." Mrs. Spencer smiled as she waved her hand around her kitchen. "It's a mite smaller, mind ya, but there's running water and a bathroom too. Matt was workin' at the Hardware Store then, and they let him work off the stuff that wasn't donated. He's gone now, and the bit that's left owin', I pay with my own money."

"What do you do?" Jim entered her warm kitchen, the whiff of fresh baking making his mouth water.

"I knit for people, and I got a big hen house, so I supply the grocer with his eggs. My son helps me a lot. Won't be long, the place'll be paid." Mrs. Spencer moved quickly about the kitchen, bringing down cups for them and filling a platter with cinnamon buns. Despite her age, she still had a litheness to her measured footsteps. She brought some freshly creamed butter to the table, the moisture still clinging to the clotted mound. "Everythin's home-made 'round here. Dig in, dig in," she encouraged, waving her hands at him.

The smell of recently perked coffee and fresh buns whetted his appetite, and Jim ate with gusto, devouring three cinnamon knots in short order. Mrs. Spencer was a gold mine of information, and by 3:00, he had all the answers he wanted. Smiling, he thanked her and bade her goodbye, his footsteps much lighter than before.

Lucy was a school teacher now. Likely, he'd still find her there. An hour later, Jim arrived at the schoolyard and let the memories wash over him. He shut off the ignition and leaned into the vehicle door, forcefully jerking it open. Slapping at his dark grey pinstriped suit jacket to release the wrinkles from the trip, Jim checked himself over in the truck's side mirror. A smile broke over his face as he angled his hat over his head. Jim swiped his hand-kerchief over his black leather shoes, restoring the shine, and hoped Lucy would welcome his new appearance.

She'd never seen him as an adult and all spruced up before.

Taking a deep breath, Jim surveyed his old stomping grounds. Funny how time seemed to have frozen here, he mused. The tire swings still hung beneath the elm tree, and the wood-paned windows still cried for paint. He noticed the roof had been repaired, and an oil tank had replaced the stacks of firewood at the side door. Some progress had been made, after all, he chuckled, yet he doubted that anything could really change the character of that building.

Nostalgia for the simpler days flooded his senses as he remembered playing softball with his friends. The boys showed off at every chance to catch the girls' attention on the school bench, whispering and giggling. His blood pounded, and his face flushed whenever Lucy glanced his way and saw him watching her.

Jim had long lost his shyness regarding women, yet he couldn't help feeling anxious about this unexpected meeting. His palms began to sweat as his heartbeat quickened. He wondered if she'd be excited to see him or whether she'd turn a cold shoulder. God knew if that happened, he would be lost again. Jim pursed his lips and forced his breath to slow down as he tried to control the various emotions spiking through his body.

A couple of young children were still playing catch in the yard and, after giving Jim a curious stare, turned back to their game. A sense of calm overcame Jim as he found himself at the crossroad he'd been fearful of facing. Today, he'd have his answers one way or another. His eyes flickered to the schoolhouse as the side door opened, and a young woman appeared.

Lucy stood with her back toward him, books loaded in one arm, a brown satchel strapped over her right shoulder, and a purse clutched precariously under her chin. More beautiful than he'd remembered and as impatient as ever. A breeze caught her navy coat, making it flare back into the doorway as she tried to close the door, causing her to grumble in frustration. Dropping her books and purse to the porch, Lucy pulled her keys out of her pocket and locked the school. She buttoned her coat before picking up her supplies and then hurried down the steps.

Jim felt his heart quicken. Lucy's hair was darker and much longer than when he'd seen her last. With her matching cloche hat and sensible shoes, she truly embodied the practical country teacher she'd always hoped she'd become. Her cheeks were as rosy as he recalled them, her lips as full as he envisioned in a thousand dreams. A trickle of fear snaked through his gut when he thought of her probable reaction to his appearance.

Maybe this was a bad idea. He and Lucy had both grown up and become different people. He'd changed dramatically from the naïve, trusting young man she'd said goodbye to. She probably wouldn't even like who he was now. For a moment, Jim felt the urge to turn and walk away. Another rejection would kill him.

As he debated his choices, he saw a young boy breaking away from his playmates and running towards her, skipping up the stairs and chattering away. The youngster charged her, grasping her thigh as his little head strained upwards, trying to catch her attention. She knelt, dropping her books once again, and wrapped her arms around the boy, swaying slightly and hugging him fiercely. His demands abated after the loving attention, then he picked up her purse and led her down the stairs.

Jim widened his eyes in wonder. He removed his new hat, fingering the rim nervously, then cleared his throat in an effort to remain calm. *Lucy was a mother*. There was no doubt in his mind. The bond was too great for that display to be one of pupil and teacher.

His heart sank. Jim was frozen to the spot as the implications slid over him. There was no use now. Lucy was married. Why hadn't Mrs. Spencer told him that? She had only mentioned her teaching position. That was all—nothing about a child or a husband. Jim recalled a glint of amusement in her eye. A flush ran up his neck as he suppressed a growl of frustration. What did that old lady have up her sleeve?

If this were her idea of a joke, he would be furious. Mrs. Spencer had seemed so friendly and encouraging. Had he known that Lucy was married and had a child, he would never have come and risked meeting her. Damn that busybody—

Frustration and disappointment whirled about inside him. Who took his place? Why? The old question squeezed his chest in a familiar pain, and suddenly Jim knew he could not leave until he got his answers. He needed to understand the reasons for her rejection, or he'd never be able to move on. Jim slapped his hat back on his head and forced his tightened lips into a welcoming smile as he approached Lucy, waiting for her to notice him.

He had to know if their love had been one-sided or forgotten as her first crush. He forced himself to approach her before he changed his mind. The autumn leaves crackled under his feet as he quickly strode towards her.

"Lucy? Lucy?" Jim broke into a jaunt. She stopped and turned, then drew the boy closer to her in an automatic protective gesture, her forehead scrunching as she tried to place who was approaching her.

"It's me. My God, Lucy - don't you remember me?" Lucy

hadn't said a single word, yet the surprise on her face was evident. She paled and seemed to waver as the child hugging her began to whine. "Mama, mama!"

"*Oui, oui ma cher, c'est rien.*" she comforted, patting his shoulder. Her voice shook, and as she took a step backward, he could see the tears forming in her eyes. She licked her lips nervously, then straightened her shoulders.

"Jim. I can hardly believe it. You're a little late, aren't you?" Her composure returned, and she turned away, walking towards town.

"Luce!" Jim raised his voice in disbelief. His eyebrows lifted as he lowered his tone and pleaded. "Stop. Please?" When Lucy leaned down to take her son's hand and quickened her step, Jim panicked and spoke louder. "Talk to me, dammit, unless you want me to make a scene."

Lucy glanced about her and saw the few remaining school children staring at her from the playground. Gossip started with the unusual around here, so a strange man running up to her and her son would be a story brought into their homes tonight. She smiled back to reassure her audience, then shrugged her shoulders and motioned him to join her. Only Jim could tell that the smile was forced. Her luminous tiger eyes were mirrors of pain and distrust, darting away from his and centering ahead of her.

"If someone has a right to be angry here, it's me," Jim growled defensively. "Why didn't you write me back? All those years, all the letters I sent you, begging you to come and join me."

"Oh sure," Lucy's lips twisted as she struggled to keep her voice calm for the audience watching them. "Liar. How can you stand there and lie to me?"

The child began to whimper again, afraid of the stranger and alarmed by his gentle mother's tone. She knelt on one knee beside him. "That's enough now, Willy. You're a big boy, don't whine. This man's a friend that I went to school with. He's been away for a very long time, and he's come to say hello. His name's Mr. Taylor. Say hello," she encouraged.

Jim made the first gesture. "Hi, Willy. Your Mama's right. I'm sorry if I scared you. I wanted to surprise her, and maybe all I did was upset both of you. How about if we go to the general store and have a treat? Then we can talk some more."

"Ok." A big smile spread across his face, replacing the fear he had first felt. Willy glanced upwards at his mother, searching for reassurance. "Is that ok, Mama?" he tacked on as an after-thought.

"I suppose so." Lucy ruffled her son's hair and produced a gentle smile to ease her son's anxiety. "Mr. Taylor and I'll sit and have coffee and talk. Maybe you'd like to have some licorice and go back to the schoolyard and share it with your friends?"

"Oh yes, Mama." Minutes later, Willy carried a small brown bag filled with the candies he chose, compliments of his mother's new friend. Not a shred of apprehension marred the boy. Licorice and the encouragement to join his friends had calmed his fears.

Lucy watched him race back to his friends and turned to Jim. "I'm glad to see you, Jim. Although, I was very angry with you for a few years. Where have you been? I'm dying to hear your excuses." Although her tone was somewhat more relaxed, her eyes revealed her bitterness.

"Long story. I rode the rails for a year, worked as a stevedore on the docks in Kingston for a while, then made my way to a smelter in Quebec where I worked producing metals for the war." Jim and Lucy walked to the café, sat at a round table near the front window, then ordered coffees before resuming the conversation. "When it ended, I took the train to Prince Albert and decided to come and see my old hometown. I don't know how long I'll be staying. It depends. I was thinking of heading west, but I needed to see you before I went any further." Jim added sugar to his coffee and stirred it slowly, his eyes downcast. He swallowed to ease the lump in his throat, then glanced into Lucy's eyes before switching the subject.

"So, you're a teacher, now? You always dreamed about becoming one. It looks like you've made a good life for yourself."

Lucy eyed him warily. "Yes, I went to Saskatoon for a year to become a teaching assistant. Around here, that's all you need. I've enjoyed working with the kids. When Mrs. Larose retired, I took over her position, and it's been great. I can take Willy to school with me anytime I need to."

"Your son looks healthy and strong. Full of mischief. Who's the lucky father?" Jim tried to keep his tone light as he saw Lucy's lips begin to tremble. He noticed her taking a deep breath, trying to calm herself. Was she scared of him?

"Marc Beaumont. His parents were friends of my father. We married six months after I returned from my course. That was over two years after you left." Her eyes were burning brightly, her voice wavering with suppressed emotion. "I waited for you to come back, Jim. I wanted to believe you."

"Wait a minute, wait a minute—don't go blaming this on me! I did write you once a week at first, then whenever I could. When I got settled in Kingston, I tried again. Every week, I wrote you. Then one day, the letters started getting returned. That's when I stopped. It was time to accept the message that you'd moved on. It almost killed me, but I had to give up trying." Jim watched his first love's face grow warm with anger.

"It can't be. You're lying. I never received one letter from you—not one." Lucy shook her forefinger at him. "I worried myself sick that first year, wondering what had happened to you." Lucy's voice rose an octave, shaking with emotion. Her head shook from side to side in righteous indignation as she continued to stab her index finger at him. "I believed you, and then you broke my heart."

"I don't understand this." Jim was at a loss for words. "Honest to God, Luce, I wrote. I begged you to write me, and then I begged you to come to me. I never received anything back, not a single word." Jim stared at Lucy, trying to absorb what she was telling him. Her face had turned pale with his story, and her eyes were gaining moisture again. "But how could I get letters from you if you'd never received mine?"

"I swear - I never got any." Lucy reached over and put her hand over Jim's. "You must have thought I was awful, breaking my promise to you."

"I guess we broke each other's hearts. I wondered why you wouldn't at least explain why you wouldn't join me, but I never received a single word. But why didn't I get *all* of my letters back? Somebody must have received them." Jim bit his top lip as he guessed what had probably happened. "Your parents! They intercepted my letters to you. They must have."

"C'mon, Jim—they wouldn't have done that."

"What other explanation is there? They wanted you to marry a Frenchman, right? I didn't fit the picture, did I? You told me yourself they would disapprove of us."

"I know, but I can't believe they would do *that*." Lucy sipped her tepid coffee to ease the dryness in her throat as she reviewed that time in her life. Her hand trembled as she put down her coffee cup. "Oh, my God."

"What? What's the matter?"

"I remember my wedding day. Papa brought me down the aisle. Before he handed me to Marc, he patted my hand and whispered that I'd made him proud by marrying within our kind. He mumbled something about the damned English. I was flustered and excited, and I let it go. I didn't even think about it again—after all, so much time had gone by. I'd honestly thought you'd forgotten about me and made a new life for yourself," Lucy's fingers tightened into a fist. "If my father did this—"

"That's the problem. Your father did know. If he opened my mail, he knew about us and how I felt about you." Frustrated, Jim slapped the table. "Dammit. I should've come back, but I was hurt, and pride wouldn't let me after a while. I almost didn't come today."

"I'm glad you did. I've always felt bad about us. I'm mad as anything at my Papa, though. Wait until I see him." Lucy's voice dropped to a growl.

"What's done is done. You're married now, and Willy looks like a loving handful. But at least now you'll know I hadn't abandoned you. I kept my word." He looked away from her, cleared his throat, and tried to keep his emotions in check.

Lucy reached over and covered his hand. "Jim, look at me." Lucy squeezed his hand harder so he'd look her in the eye and listen. When he raised his eyes, she continued. "I'm very pleased that you've come to see me. Willy's been my whole life for a while now. His father died in a hunting accident almost two years ago. I'm a widow."

Eyes widening in surprise and wonder, he searched her face. When he saw her lovely eyes softening, he felt the tightness easing in his chest. Could this be true? He gripped her hand tightly, speechless for a moment. A slow smile spread across her face as her incredible tiger's eyes lit up. He'd wondered if he'd ever see those gold-flecked brown eyes smile tenderly at him again. His heart seemed to warm as Lucy's expression became relaxed.

"I—I don't know what to say," Jim began slowly. "That must have been terrible for you. It can't be easy raising a child on your own. Willy must miss his father. And I'm sure you must miss him, too."

Lucy looked around her mischievously, then lowered her voice to a whisper. "To be truthful—not half as much as I missed you. Oh, he was a nice man, don't get me wrong, mais..."

"But?"

"But he wasn't you. The magic simply wasn't there."

Jim felt a thrill of desire pulse through him. Could this be happening? Could she still love him like she used to? "Then why did you marry him?" Jim covered her hand between his, stroking her palm with his thumb, feeling the softness he'd dreamed of for years, then brushed his lips against her fingers.

"I liked him. He was a nice guy, and I wanted to forget you and get on with my life. His proposal offered me a way out. An escape. It was fine." Lucy shrugged her shoulder. "We got along well, and he gave me Willy." Jim noticed Lucy's cheeks blush as his lips touched her skin.

"God, Luce, I love you! If you think you could feel the same way again, we'll get this all straightened out, and then I'm taking you with me. We're going west and starting a fresh new life." Jim looked at her excited, smiling face and knew that she'd follow him this time. "I want to kiss you so badly," Jim whispered.

She giggled happily at him and stood up from the arborite table. "Well, let's go get Willy, and you can come for dinner at my place. Then we'll see about the rest."

Jim threw two bits on the counter, picked up her books, and followed her outside. She called Willy to join them, and they walked the few blocks to her home. Inside the older imitation Victorian home, she drew the curtains on the tall, narrow sitting room windows and took their jackets.

Jim looked about and set to lighting the oil-burning furnace nestled in the central hallway. He listened to Willy's chatter and Lucy's busy preparations for dinner. They had a few things to iron out together, but their way would be clear. Jim smiled contentedly. For the first time in many years, he felt whole. He listened to Lucy rummaging in the ice box while Willy questioned his mother about Jim's presence. Jim entered the slowly warming kitchen and thanked his lucky stars. A family—at last.

AFTER DINNER, Jim offered to wash the dishes while she prepared Willy for bed. When asked where Jim would sleep, Lucy had her son put a pillow and blankets on the couch. She sent Willy to get into his pajamas, then went to the hall closet and retrieved two photo albums.

"I read Willy a few short stories every night, so make yourself at home," Lucy said. "Not sure if you want to see these, but this is what I've been up to since you left. I'm usually good for at least two stories before Willy falls asleep. You probably have a half hour to kill."

"Sure, I'd love to. And I'd better bring in my bag for the night. Take your time." Jim winked at her, enjoying the flush flooding her face, her bright eyes betraying a hint of nervousness. As he settled in the rocking chair, Jim listened to the melodic voice he had carried in his heart for many years. It was as warm and loving as he remembered it, and Jim almost had to pinch himself to believe he was right here with her. After a few minutes, he decided he'd better get his luggage before he started looking at her albums.

Opening the door, Jim saw headlights approaching. He sprinted down the porch steps towards his truck as another vehicle suddenly veered towards his and stopped, pebbles spitting up as it braked abruptly. He stopped in his tracks. What the hell?

The truck door slammed, and a tall man strode towards him. Jim could feel the hatred towards him and squinted ahead to determine what was happening. "Can I help you?" He made his voice strong and confident to hopefully halt this man's approach.

"Help me? Yeah, you can help me, alright. Get the hell out of here, you knucklehead! You've got no business being here. My daughter's a married woman now, a teacher with a child. She doesn't need you." Mr. Belanger spat into the dirt, showing his obvious opinion of him.

"You're right in one way. She has a wonderful son, but she's no longer married. She's a widow. And an adult. She invited me here, and I'm staying, whether you like it or not." Jim kept his voice calm and confident. He would not be bullied by this man who had tried to ruin their lives for almost ten years.

"You son of a bitch. I got rid of you before, and I'll do it again. Do you think she's going to pick you over me?"

Jim could see Lucy's father's hands clenching into a fist. This argument wasn't the way he wanted to start this relationship. "Hold on, hold on. We both want Lucy to be happy. I don't think she'll be very pleased if we're fighting against each other. Why don't you come in, and we can talk between the three of us?"

"I told you to take a powder! There's no discussion here. You're not sleeping under that roof tonight, I'll tell you that much. The only way that's going to happen is over my dead body."

"You need to calm down, sir. I've done well for myself since I left here. I've got a good nest egg behind me, and I'll be able to look after Lucy and the boy. We're going to make a great future for ourselves."

"Like hell you will." Mr. Belanger stomped within a foot of Jim's face and growled. "Last chance. Get your ass out of here. Now."

"Not going to happen. I won't throw the first punch, but I *will* defend myself. And I hardly think that would be a fair match." Jim's solid frame only emphasized the lean and older man.

Wrong thing to say, Jim thought as he received a square punch in the jaw. For a scrawny older man, he still packed a punch. Jim heard his fury growing as he panted another warning. "You may be younger than me, but I got ways to even the score. So, do yourself a favor and hit the road. Forget about this place and Lucy. She's *never* going to be yours."

"She would've been *mine* years ago if you'd have given her my letters. That child would be *my* child, so quit trying to give me the bum rap. You're the cause of a lot of heartache for Lucy and me for years." Jim stepped towards the older man, his chest bumping his and moving him backward. "You really want to do this? To prove what? That she'll listen to you and stay here and be Daddy's little girl?" Now Jim's breathing was coming quicker, and his temper was beginning to show.

"She'll stay. And she'll do what I tell her and send you packing. I didn't burn those letters for nothing. The best thing I did was send them back 'return to sender.' It took a while, but you finally gave up." Mr. Belanger's top lip curled as he snarled. "The smartest thing I've ever done is get rid of you."

"You're not rid of me yet, old man. Not by a long shot. You better get on home to your wife before someone gets hurt. Lucy, the boy, and I will come and see |you and your wife tomorrow. If you want Lucy to stay in your life, we better find a way to get along."

When Lucy's father swung his fist at him again, Jim feinted left and let his right arm block his fist, then shoved the bully away from him. Mr. Belanger lost his balance and dropped to the ground. Now he resembled an old banty rooster ready to fight to the death. He hopped to his feet and dove head first into Jim's chest, landing a punch to his kidneys before Jim again pushed him away. The sweat ran freely across the older man's face. For a brief moment, Jim wondered if he'd worked himself up for a heart attack.

"Enough, mon dit! Papa, what the hell are you doing?" Lucy ran down the steps and pushed herself between the two men she loved.

"I'm doing what I've done before—I'm going to get rid of this piece of useless flesh. He's not going to ruin your life. I forbid it. You tell him to grab his stuff and get lost. Now!"

Lucy looked between the two of them. "Is that true then? Jim told me he mailed me letters. Lots of them. Then he started getting them returned. You're the one who did that?" Lucy's eyes were beginning to water. Jim knew she'd been hoping that what happened to the letters was some kind of mistake within the post office. Her voice began to tremble as the implications set in. "Did Mama know?"

"Of course, your mama knew. She didn't argue. She knew what was best for our family. Marc was a good husband until he went and got himself killed. He was one of us. Willy understands us when we speak French, and when he wants to, he's good at talking French. That's important, Lucy. You can't tell me you didn't love Marc."

"Yes, I cared very much for Marc, and our heritage is important, Papa. But it's not the most important thing." Now Lucy's eyes were dry and had taken on a stern glare. "Honesty's the most important quality in life. *Love and honesty*. I thought that's what we had together, but now I know that's not true. You better go home, Papa."

"What? You better think twice, *ma fille*. You send me away now, and you're done. You make your bed, you lie in it —without your mother or me. Or any of the family. Is that what you want?" Her papa had stilled, but his low, gravelly voice threatened his daughter.

Lucy stood with her arms crossed and slowly sidled backward to stand close to Jim. Her papa scowled at each of them, sending daggers to both. "Be careful what you wish for, Lucy. Your family's your whole life. You belong with us."

"No, Papa. I belonged with you as a child. I'm a grown woman capable of making her own choices. I've pined for Jim for almost ten years, so you can bet I'm not letting him out of my sight. So, *you* better think twice."

Lucy's eyes glared at her father, her voice rising an octave. "I'm not Mama and won't be told what to do. Do you want Willy and me in your life or not? I hope so, but it's your choice."

Lucy looked away from her father's face, his mouth still open in surprise. She linked her arm to Jim's and hugged him. "Be careful what *you* wish for, Papa. Jim and I are planning a future together. You can accept it and be part of it, or not. This time, I'm making my own choices with full knowledge of the *truth*. The next step's yours."

Mr. Belanger's fierce glare flickered back between Jim and Lucy before he spat onto the ground again. Without a word, he turned and stomped back to his truck, roaring the engine to life. He ground the gear into reverse, slammed into first, then tore back into the night.

Jim wrapped his arms around the love of his life, murmuring endearments as he felt her shudder with suppressed emotions. "Thank you, *ma cherie*. You showed a lot of grit, standing up to your papa like that. No one should have to choose between people they love, but I'm glad you chose me." Jim pulled back and lifted her chin, drinking in each feature of her face. Tenderly, he kissed her lips, tasting the sweet promise of a lifetime of tomorrows. "I'll make you happy, I swear it. I love you with all my heart."

"I love you too. And I'm glad I know the whole truth. Whatever happens down the road, you have to promise always to be honest with me. Even if it's bad news, we can work anything out together."

"I promise. Maybe by tomorrow, your papa will calm down. Maybe your mom will convince him to bend. I had hoped to go to BC, but we could postpone that for a few years if you want." Jim knew her heart was breaking from the deception, and he would do anything to bring reconciliation between them and her family. He lowered his lips to her hair, then nuzzled his way down to her lips, kissing her gently. Now wasn't the time to push, but simply to be her rock.

"I know my papa. There won't be a compromise. As of tonight, I won't be a subject of conversation in his home again. I'll have some loyalty from Therese and maybe Raymond. Definitely not Emile, though. He's the spitting image of my papa. Mama will send me messages via Therese, but she won't cross Papa."

"I'm sorry, Luce. I wish it hadn't happened this way." Jim turned and held her arm in the crook of his, then climbed the stairs back into her home. "We'll figure it out. I promise I'll do my best to make sure you never regret what you've given up for me."

"I know. I feel sorry for you too. My father rejected you twice for no good reason, breaking my heart and making me angry. No more. I'll spend the rest of my life with you, and we'll make up for lost time, loving each other." Lucy stood on her tiptoes and kissed Jim soundly. "You'll never doubt me again."

Once inside, the two of them sat at the kitchen table, where Lucy poured each a shot glass of whiskey. "Wait a moment. I've got a surprise for you." Her eyes danced with mischief as she skipped across the kitchen to the bedroom area. Jim heard drawers opening and closing, then a giggle. She reappeared with her hands held behind her back. "Pick a hand."

Jim couldn't help smiling at the anticipatory light in her eyes. He pointed to her left hand. "That's the winner."

"You're right. It is." Lucy brought out her clenched hand that hid its' contents. "Open it."

Jim grinned, then took her hand, slowly removing each finger until the content was exposed. "Awe. Lucy. Perfect."

Lucy held the gold wedding band that Jim's father had left him. She had safeguarded it all these years. She saw the moisture in his eyes and leaned forward, kissing his forehead. "I never gave up hope completely. I've always believed that miracles can happen."

"Yes, and here's proof." Jim took the ring, slipped it on

her finger, and then kissed it. "Soon, my darling, there'll be vows to go with it."

Lucy picked up the two shot glasses and handed one to her beloved. "To us. Forever."

Jim clinked his glass to hers and repeated the vow.

Forever, together at last.

CHAPTER 10

J im folded up the well-worn maps of British Columbia and the provincial incentives to have Canadians move west in the post-war boom. He couldn't wait to share this information with his friend Keith and slipped them into his leather pouch. Who would've thought that the unlikely friendship between a returning soldier and himself would have deepened into a brotherly bond?

After spending a week with Lucy's sister as he and Lucy sorted out their respective pasts, Jim made contact with his school friends and spent another two weeks at the Madsen's, where he and his dad had lived. Almost a month after he left Keith in Prince Albert, he was back on the train to reunite and make travel plans with him.

Unmistakable affection flowed between the two as they back-slapped each other and caught up with their news. "Well, I'll be damned. I was beginning to wonder if I'd see you again. How did it go with your girl?"

"Great. We had so many lies to untangle. It turns out Lucy's father never gave her the letters I sent. She thought I had forgotten *her*. She married a man her father approved of and had a child, a boy they named Willy."

"I'm sorry to hear that, Jim. That's awful news." A frown wrinkled Keith's forehead. "Although now that you know the truth, you can move on. That's what you wanted, right?"

"True. Although there's a twist to the story—Lucy's husband died in a hunting accident, and she's a widow now. She's a teacher in the same school we attended together. Her son named Willy's almost five years old and looks exactly like her."

"Tough for her and the kid, but I'll bet that was the best news you could've hoped for. So, what's the plan? Are you sticking around for a while, or are you ready to head West?" Keith lit a cigarette and dragged deeply. He lifted the pack, offering one to Jim, who shook his head.

"I'm going to stay until the school year's finished. I've told Lucy about you and our plans to head to British Columbia. The best news, though, is that she still loves me. She's agreed to come with me after we get married."

"Congratulations!" Keith grabbed Jim's hand and pumped it several times, genuinely pleased to see a positive outcome for his friend. "When will the wedding bells ring?"

"Probably in March. Then she'll need the spring to put things in order and sell her home. She's also responsible for interviewing and training a replacement. I'm hoping we can leave by late May or early June. By the way, would you do me the honors and be my best man? If we head West together, I'd sure like you to be part of our family."

"Of course, although I'll have to leave right after the wedding. The logging outfits in Port Alberni will be hiring for the busy summer season. I want to be there as soon as I can. Do you have a problem with that?"

"No, of course not. But are you sure that's where you want to go?"

"That's all I've heard since I've been here, is the boom in the logging industry there. Lots of work and good money."

"I know. I've heard the same thing. The forestry mills are advertising in the newspaper, trying to coax us prairie chickens to move there. But that's not the only place to go. Have you ever been to a mill town? It's a lot different than living on the prairies."

"It might be good for a change. Unless you've got something better up your sleeve?"

"Lucy belongs to a teaching federation. They sent her a list of remote schools in BC looking for teachers when she gave her notice. We've talked about the opportunities. We're not sure we're ready for big city life. Lucy's used to a simpler lifestyle. We'll try Port Alberni, but if that doesn't work out, we'll look at communities on the west coast around Bella Coola and Prince Rupert."

"But what's there for us guys?" Keith asked.

"There's forestry there, too, and great fishing opportunities. The interior of the province has a lot of agriculture. It was cheap too. We could get a few sections of land to farm and not break the bank. Or stay on the coast and look at commercial fishing. You said you loved it. What do you think?"

"I dunno. I automatically thought about the lumber mills and logging operations. Something different to try. Although you're right, I've always enjoyed working on the water. It's in our blood. My great grandparents were from Norway, so they came to Canada, lured by the land offers and the fact that the fishing prospects were unbelievable."

"We've got time to figure it out. I have a map we can

study. Maybe we can do both. Try one, and if we don't like it, go to the other."

"No use making a hasty decision, alright. As I'm going first, I'll head to Port Alberni and see the place myself. I'll write and let you know what I think of it. I might as well make some good money while I'm waiting for you to arrive."

"Ok. In the meantime, I'll double-check my information, and then we can decide once we get together. You might love it enough that you won't want to go anywhere else."

"True," Keith smirked.

Jim saw his friend's eyes crease in amusement. "What's so funny? I thought you'd be interested in checking other opportunities too."

"Of course. But I've got my eye on a woman here, and if I can convince her that I'm truly crazy about her, I'm hoping you won't be the only married man heading west."

Jim's eyes widened. What the heck? This man who flirted with every skirt near him had fallen in love? In a month?

"You can't be serious. I thought you liked having a variety to choose from. I could've sworn you'd be a confirmed bachelor. She must be some dish."

"Oh yeah. Bea's got spunk with a great sense of humor. She's got a great attitude and always a quick response for everyone. I'm sure people go there solely to listen to Bea's lively wit when handling us returning soldiers." Keith's eyes became lovesick as he tried to explain his woman. "She's cheeky without being rude. Bea can slap wandering hands while giving another man a wink as she serves another person's meal— without losing track of a conversation. I liked that. A lot."

"Sounds like trouble to me." Jim watched the sparkle in

his friend's eye and wondered if Keith had bitten off more than he could chew.

"Probably. I don't think I've ever seen Bea upset, yet she's got plenty of reason to be. Her fiancé was killed in Italy during the war. She's very independent and is determined to make something of her life."

"Good heavens, she must be a spitfire. You might have picked a handful there. When can I meet her?"

"She doesn't work Sundays, but she'll be there tomorrow morning. How about if we go for breakfast before I head to work? If we're lucky, we can arrange to get together later."

"You're on. Do you think your landlady would have room for another boarder for a week or so? I want to do some banking while I'm here, then look around."

"I'm sure she can find something for you. Won't be fancy, but it'll be clean."

"That's all I need. Now tell me more about this lady." Jim walked along the street and pointed to a cafe where they could grab lunch and catch up. Keith was gesturing wildly, explaining his accidental meeting with Bea that almost caused a riot in her café.

It turns out that having two girlfriends at the same time was a recipe for a catfight. When Emily saw Keith having breakfast with a buxom redhead named Yvonne, who was well known as a loose woman, her response was immediate and drastic. Stomping into the café, she strode straight to their table, picked up Keith's plate, and threw it in his face. Of course, Yvonne responded by yelling and threw her glass of tomato juice at her. Keith tried to intervene and calm the situation, apologizing to both. The tumultuous scene settled when Bea and the owner came into the picture, grabbing both women by the arm and hustling them out the door.

Returning to the table to clean up the debris, Bea had a

few choice words for him, calling him a womanizer and a cad. Keith was swiping at the mess on the table, trying to help and apologize, but the owner hustled him out the door. He left a ten-spot tip at the register to compensate for the extra work he was responsible for and disappeared. As Keith relived the scene over the next few days, he saw himself in Bea's eyes and didn't like what he saw. This wasn't Europe celebrating the end of the war, where many men and women were ecstatic and threw caution to the wind. This was home, where reputations mattered.

"How did you get Bea to even talk to you afterward? You'd think she'd have steered a wide berth whenever you were around." Jim was wiping the tears of laughter from his eyes as his friend recounted the event. It felt so good to be happy, to laugh again from deep down in his gut. Only Keith could get into a situation like that and quickly turn it to his advantage.

"Flowers. Every day. Just a bloom or two from the florist. It cost me a bundle to take a taxi to pick them out, but I figured drastic times called for drastic measures. I'd go into the café with it for Bea. The first few days, she laughed at me and then handed them to one of the other waitresses. She ignored me totally, spending time with other customers."

As Keith recounted his courtship, it was evident that Bea's reluctance to become involved with another man was the challenge he needed to set his sights on her. Keith gained employment at a hardware and tack shop, where his organizational skills soon endeared him to the owners. He lived in a boarding house close by and spent his time off trying to catch Bea's interest, going so far as to join the Anglican Church she was a member of.

"After work yesterday, I cleaned up and went to the café.

My boss told me she always finished work by 4:00 on Saturdays. At least he seems to think we'd make a good match."

"And it worked? I'm surprised. That's darn quick. I've been away less than a month, yet you're hooked already?"

"Yup. She saw me at church the Sunday before and has kept an eye on me ever since. I've been on the straight and narrow since the catfight, so I think she knows I'm interested. After church this morning, we talked for half an hour before her friends pulled her away. Now I need to convince her that I've changed. Maybe you can help?"

"Maybe. Does Bea know that you and I've talked about moving to BC?"

"Not yet. I thought that would be something you could mention when we get together. Tell her about Lucy. They'd have a lot in common. From what my boss has said, Bea has dreams for the future. I hope I can be part of it." Keith elbowed Jim. "What do you think? Would you put a good word in for me, help me change her mind?"

JIM COULD SEE THE ROCKY MOUNTAINS' foothills approaching as they traversed Alberta's plains. The setting sun had cast a pastel tint onto the tall, craggy peaks still partially covered with snow and turned the sky into various shades of mauve. He'd never seen anything as beautiful as the vista before him. Jim looked at his small family sleeping soundly on the uncomfortable seat in the passenger section. He would do whatever it took to make a secure future for them. Their love for each other would support this new adventure into a solid and joyful life. With that thought, Jim closed his eyes finally and slept, the sounds of the rails reverberating within him, promising a brighter future just as it had all those many years ago.

The fragrant aroma of coffee awakened his senses first, then the rustling and murmurs of fellow passengers registered, as excited gasps of awe brought him fully alert. Surrounding him were towering mountains, massive cliff faces, and deep green forests edging the rail line. He glanced at Lucy. "Wow—can you believe this? How long have you been awake?"

Lucy smiled. "About an hour or so. Spectacular scenery, isn't it? Ready for some coffee?" She poured him a cup from a thermos she had refilled in the dining car, then gently nudged Willy.

"Willy, Willy. Wake up, honey. I saw some mountain goats on the cliff—you should see their big horns." As Willy rubbed his eyes and yawned, he searched for them and began to laugh.

"They've got curly horns, Mama! Why are they so big? Why are they up on those rocks?" Willy began bouncing on the seat, his hands glued to the window as he searched the mountainous cliffs around them. His chatter was at least an octave higher than usual, making his parents exchange cheerful glances and chuckles. They knew his curiosity and his questions would be ongoing for a while.

As they marveled at the size and extent of the mountain range, the train passed between the peaks, following a narrow white-water river along the valley floor. The extreme terrain made them wonder about the ingenuity, the planning, and the sacrifice it took for this rail line to exist. The many wooden trestles and tunnels were mind-boggling. Even Jim's adventures through Ontario to Quebec were nothing compared to this natural cathedral and its challenges.

LYNN BOIRE

"I've never seen anything like this, Lucy. It's unbelievable. Look at the girth of those trees – there must be enough
lumber in these trees to build everyone a home in the whole
world. I can't wait to see how they transport those monsters
to market and turn them into lumber in the mills. This trip
is probably the best adventure I've ever been on." Jim
leaned over and kissed his wife, wrapping an arm around
her as he surveyed the beauty around them. "I'm the luck-
iest man alive having you and Willy by my side."

Lucy's eyes sparkled as they shared the hope of a
brighter future. "I wouldn't miss this for the world. Nobody
will ever separate us again. We'll have a wonderful life
together." She tucked into Jim's shoulder, hugging him.
Willy snuggled between them, wanting to be included, but
soon wriggled out of it, scrambling onto the seat to see more
of the new world around him. Surreptitiously, Lucy patted
her tummy bump. She couldn't wait to surprise her husband
and Willy.

The amazingly tall evergreens forested the mountains
wherever there was a foothold for their roots. Nothing came
close to comparing these massive tree trunks to their
Saskatchewan jackpines. His experience with harvesting
timber was limited to the relatively stunted growth of evergreens in northern Saskatchewan or the already milled
planks harvested in Ontario that he had loaded onto
container ships for export. He shook his head with wonder
and excitement. No doubt about it, he was in for the experience of a lifetime.

The train slowed and screeched to a stop, steam hissing
as the conductors calmed the rush of anxious travelers eager
to be on solid ground. The small town of Cranbrook was
their first stop in BC. They stretched their legs and walked
about, letting Willy run his heart out, yelping with exuber-

ance over anything and everything. Lucy went into the General Store and bought some fresh bread, cheese, and a few green apples to bring back on the train. She was frugal, and the less they could use the train's dining car, the better – setting up in Port Alberni would be expensive. She hoped she'd be able to get a teaching job quickly.

"Did you see that, Luce?" Jim pointed out a bulletin board filled with "Help Wanted" ads, looking for men to work in lumber camps in the Kootenay areas. But his family would have to live here, and he would be in camp for a month or two at a time, depending on its location. Tempting as the wages were, that wasn't an option for him.

Lucy nodded, aware of his promise to always be by her side. She was so blissful that she could hardly stop smiling, and it felt good. Amazingly good.

Jim watched his wife glowing with the same joy she woke up with every day since they reunited. He was never going to live away from her again. But it made him feel confident that B.C. was the place to come and work. He may not make the big money they were offering here, but in Port Alberni, he'd be home every night. Once again, he counted himself fortunate for the chance encounter with Keith.

Back on the train, they waited their turn to freshen up in the bathroom, change clothes and get comfortable again. Their eyes returned to the view, amazed by the long, deep lakes nestled between the mountain ranges and the never-ending forests as they passed through the Shuswap Lakes. There was evidence of some cleared areas on some of the gentler slopes of the mountains, where Jim guessed the camps worked once the snow melt was complete. Talking with a few other men who gathered near the back of their rail car, Jim learned some of the terminologies he'd need to be familiar with.

As the day turned to evening, the Taylor family went to the dining car and ordered dinner. The roast chicken, mashed potatoes, and vegetables were tasty, but the best part of the dinner was the coffee and apple pie afterward. Glancing over to their son, whose eyes struggled to stay open, Jim nodded to Lucy to head back to their seats. Jim picked Willy up and smiled as his son snuggled into his neck, his soft breath warm against his skin. Holding him close as Lucy set up the makeshift bed along the bench seats, Jim felt a deep contentment settle in his chest. He was part of a family now, and he hoped they'd be adding more in the years to come.

Jim watched Lucy as she gently laid their son on the blanket, removing his shoes and tucking the blanket around him. She was such a great mother. Lucy would probably repeat last night's routine rather than rouse him to get him washed for bed. He would sleep in his clothes tonight, and then tomorrow, she'd give him a sponge bath and dress him in fresh clothes. Jim watched his wife run her fingers through her son's thick curly hair, then trace her finger down his brow and over his plump rosy cheeks. She kissed him softly, then returned to sit beside him. Jim put his arm around his wife, pulled her into him, and kissed her cheek.

"We're going to have a wonderful future ahead of us, my love. I know you're already missing your sister and her family, but don't worry. We'll find a way for them to join us."

"I hope so. I can't imagine life without Therese and her family. Even Willy cried when we left Claire behind. They were almost like brother and sister."

"I know. We'll lure your family soon for a visit. Once they see the beauty and opportunity here, leaving the prairies will probably be more tempting."

"I've been praying every night for that visit to happen.

Heaven knows, there's enough work here for them. I know they'd be much happier here. Their quality of life would be far beyond what they have on the farm they lease."

"We can only hope they build the courage to try something new. Your sister will miss you just as much as you miss her. You watch. It won't take them long to decide to join us." As Lucy sighed at the dilemma, Jim stroked his wife's thick hair until he felt her body relax against him. He waited until her even breathing signaled sleep had claimed her, then placed a sweater to support her head against the corner and leaned her onto it. He spread the blanket equally between mother and son, then moved to sit across from them, watching them sleep.

As the lights dimmed in the rail car, Jim stretched his legs in front of him, folded his arms, and let his mind wander. He was confident that this new chapter in his married life would be successful. With his two loves beside him, he knew there was nothing that couldn't be overcome. The farther they traveled, the more he was convinced they had made the right choice to journey west.

After all, look what he'd accomplished so far—with money in his bank account and the support beside him, Jim knew he would find the perfect place for them. A safe haven where they could prosper and begin a legacy for the future.

Jim caught the occasional glimpse of long, narrow lakes nestled in the mountains, still covered with ice and now glowing in the moonlight. It brought back warm memories of him and his dad on their only trip together. It seemed like a hundred years ago when his father had guided him along his trapline into the Churchill Basin. Young and naïve, he'd left his hometown as an eager but inexperienced, dependent son. Jim transitioned to manhood as his father patiently taught him the necessary survival skills to live, trap, and cure skins. The icy, lonely days after his father died forged his independence and strengthened his backbone as he fumbled through the frosty spring and returned home.

Looking back, Jim realized that both the physical demands and mental uncertainty were responsible for making him resilient and determined to find a future for himself. It took several years, but gradually he began to understand that failure was his opportunity to strike out in a different direction. Now, he wasn't afraid when mapping out a plan for his family. A 'Y' in the road didn't need to cause anxiety and fear. It could be spelling new prospects.

All in all, when Jim looked back on his adventures, he felt good about his decisions and the experiences he gained. All the trials of his travels had made him a stronger person. Finally, he was back in the arms of the most important person in his life, Lucy.

Lucy and Willy were the reasons he lived for, the guideline for every future decision he'd ever make.

Jim lifted his cap and ruffled his hair, then glanced at his inspirations. Lucy's head lay on her folded sweater against the window. The gentle jostling of the train continued to entice a deep sleep, painting a picture of peaceful perfection. Jim's sense of responsibility swelled with pride. He made a personal pledge they would enjoy life together and always be thankful for each other. He knew it had been hard for Lucy to leave her family, so Jim was determined to do whatever it took to bring her older sister and her family to live with them. Filled with purpose, he slowly relaxed and let his mind rest while the train's rhythm lulled him to deeper sleep.

The morning arrived full of chatter from passengers as they stretched, freshened up, and gathered their possessions. The flat farmland of the Fraser Valley stretched before them, and the conductor announced stops at Abbotsford, Fort Langley, New Westminister, then, finally, the CPR station in Vancouver. The next step would be to arrange transportation to the Black Ball Ferry, bringing them across the thirty-mile crossing of the Strait of Juan de Fuca to Vancouver Island.

After disembarking the train and gathering their possessions, Jim purchased bus tickets, and the family waited across the street from the rail terminal for their bus to arrive. The flurry of busy Vancouver streets was noisy but invigorating. In the background, the mountains loomed with the famous Lions' Head peaks guarding over the Jewel of the Pacific. Both Jim and Lucy were busy checking the stunning scenery. They scarcely spoke to each other until their baggage was loaded and they were in their seats. Their eyes were jumping from one new vista to another, beguiling them with the wonder of a beautiful June morning on the coast.

Within minutes, the first views of the ocean and the ferry took their breath away. Neither had realized the size of the ferry they were boarding or the expanse of the sea behind it. Pictures simply didn't do it justice. They smiled nervously at each other and squeezed each other's hands.

"Mama, what's that? What is it? Are we going on that boat?"

"It's a ship, Willy, and because cars can go on it too, it's called a ferry. And yes, we are going on it. Won't that be fun?"

"Are we going to sleep on it, like the train?"

"No, we'll only be on it for a few hours until we reach Nanaimo. That's the first city we'll see on Vancouver Island."

Willy squirmed about, not worried about the next city, simply anxious to disembark from the bus and explore the ship. Any concerns they had that Willy would be afraid were quickly abandoned as Lucy grabbed his hand to stop him from racing off the bus. Their belongings would remain on board until they reached the Nanaimo depot. They were free to walk around the decks, breathing the salty, fresh air. There was a lightness to their steps and excitement that was impossible to contain.

"Watch the men on the dock, Willy. See the thick rope they're untying? We'll be leaving soon." As the captain warned of the ship's warning whistle, Lucy grabbed Willy's hand and cautioned him not to be alarmed.

Willy pulled his hand from his mother's and covered his ears, jumping up and down enthusiastically. Soon after, he giggled at the seagulls swirling and following the ferry. They circled the outside decks several times, releasing the pent-up energy of the past three days of train travel. Eventually, the family settled in a cafeteria area for lunch. Lucy sat down heavily. Her eyes sparkled with happiness, but the shadows beneath attested to the fatigue she was feeling.

"Are you alright, ma cherie?" Jim asked in a rare quiet moment when Willy was eating French fries.

"Never better, my darling." Lucy reached over and took Jim's hand, placing it on her stomach. "Although, the best will arrive in six months."

Jim's eyes widened as his eyebrows jumped almost to his hairline. "What? You're in the family way?"

"Yes, my love. I've been saving this announcement as a surprise to start our new life. Congratulations, Papa!"

"Lucy, I'm so happy. Having our baby is a perfect blessing to start our new life. Thank you, Lord."

∾

SCANNING the arrivals at the Departure Bay terminal, Keith squeezed Bea's hand and pointed. "There. Wouldn't you know they'd be the last ones off the ferry?" The bustle of passengers leaving the ferry had them worried that perhaps their friends hadn't made the 2:00 sailing as planned. That would mean waiting another two hours until the following ferry came.

"Remember when we arrived, how exhausted we were? I think I slept for two days straight. And I'll bet Lucy will too." Bea waved her arms high over her head while Keith let out a shrill whistle to capture their attention.

"You ole dog—it took you long enough to get here." Keith laughed as he shook his friend's hand vigorously. "The missus and Willy held you back some, I'm figuring." Keith's eyebrows wiggled suggestively.

Bea smacked her husband's shoulder. "Enough, quit whistling dixie. Take Willy and help Jim with the luggage while I take Lucy outside to the car." Bea leaned forward and bussed Lucy on both cheeks, noting the tears of relief and happiness in her eyes. "You poor woman, you must be exhausted. Even without a child, I was bushed when we arrived here. Is everything alright?"

"Yes. Overwhelming actually. It's very different here than the prairies. The mountains, the trees—even the ferry ride was frightening at first. Everything seems larger than life here. Do you ever get used to it?"

"It took me a while. At first, I felt claustrophobic with the mountain ranges on the Island and the huge trees that block out the sun sometimes. And the rain! No wonder they have such large trees." Bea shook her head as she remembered last fall when it rained for two weeks straight. "When it finally stopped snowing the first time, I ran outside and played in almost three feet of it. I felt like a young kid, excited with the wonder of it." Bea shrugged her shoulder, "but a month later, I wanted to see the end of it—I was tired of shoveling it and scared of the slippery roads. At least this winter, I'll know what to expect." Bea's eyes twinkled at the thought. "I might have to take up knitting to keep me sane."

"Oh, Lord. Willy's going to love it. I can see it now. He'll want toboggans instead of bicycles." Lucy brightened at the thought of her son frolicking in the deep snow. "I'll probably miss the sunny days. Even in deep winter, the sun was bright and welcoming although it was icy cold."

"True. My biggest adjustment was missing the horizon and knowing the time of day. Back home, I could see the sun crack the horizon in the east and slip down in the west at night. I could tell the time of day by the sun's position. In Prince Albert, rolling hills were the highest elevation I was used to encountering. It doesn't work that way here."

Bea shrugged her shoulders at all the new experiences she'd faced. "I must warn you about the road we'll be driving to Port Alberni. There's not more than a mile or two of straight road, and it's all curves. The first time we drove there, I was a nervous wreck when we circled Cameron Lake and started up the final stretch of mountain road. Keith's a good driver and kept his speed low. He'd pull over and let the traffic by so I didn't panic. It's taken some grit, but I'm enjoying our new life now. Always something new to discover."

"Good to hear, then I know I'll be fine too. At least I know you and Keith. I won't feel completely alone."

"Keith and I are trying to start a family, but we haven't been lucky yet. We'll be each other's families. If ever you need a break, I'd be glad to babysit Willy, and you can coach me through my pregnancy."

"Thanks, Bea. I'd love that. I'm already missing my sister,

Therese. By the way, have you been watching the newspaper for a house for us? We feel blessed that you've asked us to stay with you, but we don't want to be a pain in your neck. Jim wants to buy a home as soon as he becomes a steady employee."

"We've been keeping an eye out for you. There's a lot of new construction, with subdivisions in every direction. You'll have a lot to choose from once Jim gets steady work. I'm sure he'll be working within a week."

"Probably. Jim's anxious to get established. Where's Keith working?"

Bea chuckled. "He's tried a few things already. After pulling lumber off the green chain for a month after we first arrived, he decided to quit busting his chops there and transferred over to Sproat Lake Division log sort. He's always loved the water, so being a boat operator that sorts the logs dumps is right up his alley. Once the logs are divided into sections by species, they drag the booms to the mills for processing. He loves it. They're always screaming for help. If Jim wants to work there, he'll tell his boss."

"Hmm. Jim's never taken to water before. When he was younger, he worked on the docks loading lumber on ships, but he's not anxious to return to that. I think he's hoping for logging or construction work. I don't think Jim cares what he does as long as he enjoys it and comes home every night." A sheen of perspiration appeared on Lucy's face, and she weaved slightly. She held her arm out to Bea to catch her balance.

Bea saw the classic signs of fainting and held Lucy tightly. "Hook your arm in mine, and I'll get you to the car, then you can rest. I have a thermos of water and a thermos of coffee in the car. That might help." Bea's soothing voice seemed to calm Lucy as they slowly walked through the terminal and into the parking lot. Bea helped make her comfortable in the backseat and then climbed in beside her, offering her a cup of water. As the color returned to her cheeks, Bea relaxed.

THE DOORS CLOSED behind Jim as he stepped off the crummy that picked up and dropped off the loggers at their homes. It was a long day, twenty minutes to drive to the muster station, where the men would divide into their crews. Another half-hour drive up the steep gravel roads to the side of the currently logged mountain. Eight full hours of back-breaking work, then the long ride back home made for at least a ten-hour work day. Jim was glad he had some experience falling and limbing trees in Saskatchewan, even if those trees had been less than half the size of the evergreens logged here.

He adjusted the pair of corked boots across his shoulder and swung his lunch kit happily as he approached the two-bedroom home he and Lucy had bought on Tenth Avenue. The weekend was here, and he'd have the time and energy to enjoy his family. A sprinkling of snow fell when they left their marshaling yard, which brought mixed reactions from the men. There'd be a winter layoff soon. Only men with the most seniority would get to continue logging in the lower elevations. Thankful for his healthy bank account made in Rouyn Noranda, Jim was glad he wasn't one of them. He felt sympathy for the men who weren't financially secure, knowing the strain unemployment brought them.

Willy watched out the window for his dad, searching through the dim light cast from the porch. He ran to the side door and threw it open, reaching for his dad's lunch kit and chattering a mile a minute. It never failed to warm Jim's heart to see the light waiting for him and his son's enthusiastic welcome. He dropped his spiked boots into a heavy cardboard box to stop them from scratching the linoleum, then hung his jacket up.

"Where's mom?" Jim's nose detected something simmering on the stove, but Lucy was nowhere in sight. The radio was on the local station, CJAV, and the news was broadcasting.

"Laying down. Mom said to tell you the food's ready, and she made some biscuits for us too. I set the table for her, Dad. I'm her helper."

"Yes, you're a great helper. I'm going to wash up and then go in and see her before dinner. Do you still have your crayons out? You could draw her a picture while you're waiting for me."

"Ok. Mom sounds funny when she breathes, Dad."

"Don't worry. I'll check on her and give your mom some medicine if she needs it. I'll be home for the next few days, so we'll look after her together."

"I brought Mom some water. And some crackers, but she didn't eat them." Willy scrunched up his face like he usually did when he was upset.

"Good man." Jim ruffled his son's curly hair and bent to hug him, then went to the washroom and filled the sink with water. Stripping out of his work clothes, he threw them in the bathtub and freshened up to see his wife. Even though it was early, he snuck into their bedroom and dressed in his pajamas.

Lucy lay propped on two pillows. Faint blue circles around her eyes told him she'd had a tough day and was exhausted. Today was the second time she'd had trouble with her lungs this month. Since moving here, Lucy had experienced it more times than he was comfortable with. She'd never suffered from asthma in Saskatchewan, which was frightening for both of them.

Jim quietly laid beside his wife, gently wrapping an arm around her. Her labored breathing scared him. For a moment, there was complete silence in the room as her breathing stopped. Then her eyes popped open as she gasped, her breathing rapid and wheezy.

"I'm here, Luce." Jim squeezed her arm gently to reassure the panic she still felt when she lost her breath. "Slow and easy, my love. I'm right here. When was your last dose of medicine?"

Lucy held three fingers up.

"Close enough. I'll get the spray bottle and help you." Jim went to the medicine cupboard in the washroom. He took the bulbous contraption and a vial of epinephrine solution back to their bedroom. Measuring carefully, he dropped it into the nebulizer and brought it close to Lucy's nose. "You know the routine. Hold the funnel to your nose so I can spray this in it. I'll start pumping, so be ready to breathe deeply as the mist comes out. As deep as you can, sweetheart." Lucy nodded in agreement as she rubbed her chest, trying to loosen the tight muscles.

Within five minutes of breathing the vapor, the panicked look in his wife's eyes receded as her bronchial muscles relaxed and allowed more oxygen in her lungs. Lucy continued to draw in the mist for another five minutes until she felt her rapid breathing begin to slow. Ten minutes later, she was pushing the nebulizer away.

"I'm okay now. I'm glad you were here, though. I think I was beginning to scare Willy. I didn't want to take any more medication for at least another hour, so I laid down."

"Dr. Wilson recommended every four hours as needed.

If you need it before, then use it. You don't need to suffer more than necessary." Jim tucked her head into his shoulder and kissed her forehead. He gathered the materials and went to put them away and clean the nebulizer for the next session. He returned and sat beside her stroking her cheek lovingly. "What triggered the attack this time?"

"I've no idea. I took a morning dose and another small dose at lunchtime. I felt fine most of the day. Willy and I walked to the grocery store around 3:00 to pick up some fresh milk. He was skipping ahead of me, so I sprinted to catch up with him. Then I began to feel my chest tighten, and I knew it was coming again. Damn, I hate this. I've never, ever had trouble with my lungs. I don't know why it's happening now."

"I've talked to a few of the guys to see if they've had problems. It's quite common here in the winter. Overcast days, lots of rain. The fly-ash from the pulp mill gets trapped, and some people who work outside are susceptible to asthma attacks."

"Bea said the same thing. Her neighbor's daughter gets these attacks quite often too. I'm keeping my eye on Willy, but he doesn't seem to be bothered by it so far. I'll have to be more careful."

"At least in the winter. Leave the grocery shopping until the weekend, when I can drive you. Or you can give me a list, and I'll shop for you."

"You can drive me, but you're not going to shop for me. I need to get out of the house now and then. I can't stay inside all day, every day. Bea usually stops for a weekly visit and offers to bring me whatever I need if I feel poorly. I'll manage."

Jim spread his hands out in surrender. "Alright. Be careful, though, my love. It worries me to see you like this."

"I will. I promise." Lucy pushed the coverlet aside and then took Jim's hand to help her out of bed. "Good thing I made beef stew this morning. It'll be tender by now. Let me get it on the table."

"Willy's set the table already. Let me help you. Let me spoil you tonight. I'll even do the dishes."

"Mon Dieu – a man who washes dishes? What will the neighbors think?" Lucy giggled. "No, I'm feeling much stronger now. You can serve dinner, but Willy and I'll clean up. You've had a long day, too."

"Don't forget I was a bachelor for many years—I know how to clean up. Come and seat yourself, my princess, and let your man serve you dinner." Jim lightened his tone, forcing a smile to his lips and eyes. He hid the worry that had been gnawing at him. As much as they had enjoyed exploring the Alberni Valley this summer, it didn't make up for a winter like this one.

Lucy gave up her part-time position as a teacher at Alberni Elementary School in November. Too many days were cut short because of asthma attacks. Jim knew how much that had affected his wife. She loved working with students, and her inability to continue had turned her usually cheerful wife into a different person. Lucy's dedication to her pupils helped keep her mind off the loneliness she felt from the separation from her family and the grief of miscarriage she had when they first moved here.

Now, she seemed to struggle with the blues. This situation with Lucy's health wasn't what Jim had hoped their life here would be like. He had promised to give her a bright future, full of love and happiness.

Had he failed? What could he do to make things better? He enjoyed living in the forestry-centered town. The Beaufort Range surrounded them in a cocoon, while the rivers and lakes beckoned them to picnic and enjoy the crystal, clear waters. The saltwater port harbored huge ships taking their product around the world. He'd never lived anywhere as beautiful and diverse as this place.

The opportunities were exactly as Terry had described. You could quit your job one day and have another before the end of the day. And the wages were good, thanks to a strong union. But without Lucy's good health, the benefits of living here paled. After getting Willy to bed, Jim sat in the dimly lit living room and questioned his decision to move there. BC was a vast province full of different opportunities.

"I think I'd like to explore some other communities this summer, Lucy. Somewhere healthier. Get back to country living. What do you think?"

"But it's beautiful here, and we're hardly even settled. We're getting to know more people through work and church. And what about Terry and Bea? She's like a sister to me now. I don't want to lose her."

"You never know, they might come with us. I don't think Terry's committed to this valley being his whole life forever and ever. We talked about this before he and Bea got married. We were going to go our separate ways and let the other know what we'd found. Instead, we ended up staying here with them. I remember the offer you had for teaching in Prince George and other others from coastal communities. We never did check them out."

"I know, but what about you? I think it's more important that you're working at something you love. You have a whole lifetime to work. We have to find something we both enjoy. I honestly thought it was going to be here."

"Me too. Although, I have to admit I miss the cold, clear days of the prairie winters. It becomes very confining in the winter here. Low clouds, fog, and rain. Doesn't that bother you?"

Lucy knitted her fingers together and was quiet a moment. "I suppose so. It's nothing I won't get used to, though. The summers make up for it. I'm not complaining. I thought you enjoyed working here."

"I am. But that doesn't mean I won't enjoy being somewhere else either. I've done many kinds of jobs over the years. I'm not attached to any one thing except you. And what I want most is for you to have good health all year-'round. I know we can find something that'll suit us. Let's take some time this winter and look into other areas. It doesn't mean we'll go right away. We'll take our time, okay?"

"I guess so." Lucy's eyes brightened. "I can pick up the Vancouver Sun newspaper for employment ads, then go to the library and research the communities. What jobs interest you?"

"Honestly? I don't know. Let's see what strikes our fancy. We have a healthy bank account, so why not use it? I've always dreamed of owning land—not farms growing grain like we grew up on. But maybe a ranch or orchards? I'd like to own acreage to develop any way we want. Someplace where we have bright, sunny winters. I can handle the cold weather way better than the clouds and rain. What do you say?"

"I like the idea. And if we found sections of land you could work while I teach, I'll bet I could convince Therese and Leo to move with us. They're farmers through and through, and I doubt they'd ever be happy working in a mill town. Their farm is leased, and they've lived there since they married. I know she misses me terribly. If they'd have a chance at owning their property, I'm sure they'd join us."

"Alright. That's your job this winter. When I'm off for

snow, I'll help you. We'll look at a few places and see if we find something better for us. What do you think?"

"I say, yes. Will you talk to Keith and ask if he'd join us? I don't want to lose their friendship."

"I'll do that. Now that Bea's pregnant, she might be looking for something more basic than town living too." Jim pulled his wife to him, hugging her. "More than anything else, Luce –I want you to be healthy and happy and have your sister living close to you. When that happens, I'll know I've kept my promise to look after you."

EPILOGUE

1958
Bella Coola, British Columbia

Looking back, Lucy was pleased with her new life with her extended family. Jim had bought two sections of land for himself outside the small coastal community of Bella Coola. Within a year of Jim and Lucy moving there, Therese and Leo Devereau and their children, Claire and Gerard, followed from Saskatchewan. They were excited at the prospect of becoming the proud landowners of an adjoining half-section financed by Jim and Lucy.

Another year later, Keith and Bea sold their home in Port Alberni for a hefty profit and joined them with their young daughter. They had taken a chance to follow a dream leading to a modest and healthier lifestyle in the small northwest village on coastal British Columbia. Since then, Lucy had suffered significantly fewer asthma attacks, and even those were usually due to exposure to extreme cold. The three families had grown into a tightly knit support group that Jim hadn't ever experienced.

When Bea and Keith had first joined them in Bella Coola, Lucy recognized the fear on her face when Bea realized how isolated they were. Keith was excited at the prospect of owning his commercial fishing vessel, away fishing long days and weeks from the spring to early fall. During the winter, he milled lumber from the evergreens that he and Jim felled in the summer. The men were busy and excited about their new lives.

Although Bea was busy with their two-year-old daughter, Hannah, she often told Lucy that she wasn't sure she meant to be a full-time mother. Bea was born to work. She'd been working in a restaurant since she was fifteen and missed the social interaction as well as the paycheck that kept her spirit independent. When Hannah reached grade school, Bea was ready. With the money she'd squirreled away, she'd convinced her husband that a bakery was exactly what Bella Coola needed.

With recipes fine-honed while experimenting with her family, the Taylors and the Devereaus, Bea settled on a menu of fresh goods that would appeal to most residents. Bea's menu provided something for everyone, from hearty brown and rye loaves of bread to light, fluffy croissants and doughnuts. On Fridays, Jim was always first in line for deep-fried Bannock served with tiny jars of local wild fruit jam and fresh, strong coffee.

Lucy's eldest sister, Therese, was an expert in bread-making and had joined Bea when sales quickly skyrocketed. When Therese received her first-ever paycheck, the joyous expression on her face was priceless. Even Lucy stepped in to work the counter sales in the summer when her job as the school principal paused. Life was good. Bea's quick wit and commitment to excellent service learned so young in life drew customers in, and the mouth-watering menu kept them coming back.

Three years ago, Bea announced her wishes to expand her business by adding a coffee shop. Jim and Keith added an addition that would serve up to twenty people. Delicacies like Cardamon Almond Tarts or Oslo Kringle, a variation of a cream puff drizzled in icing and sprinkled with slivered toasted almonds, were recipes from Keith's Norwegian grandmother and were a favorite in town. She listened to her clients' preferences and adapted her menus to return for more mouthwatering treats. Bea's Bakery opened early at 8:00 a.m. and closed by 3:00 when her daughter would walk there after school and enjoy a treat while the cafe was getting ready for the following day.

Lucy waved her fingers in a silent goodbye as she left the bakery/coffee shop. Even though she knew what this date meant, Bea was too busy to snag for a conversation today. On Thursdays, Hannah attended riding lessons at their neighbors and would go to Lucy's afterward and wait for her mom. She'd see Bea when she picked up her daughter. Then they could hold each other tight and remember.

Six years ago today, Jim and Lucy's precious daughter, Denise, passed away. Complications from polio had weakened the four-year-old until her heart gave up the fight. Lucy thought she'd never feel anything but the sharp edge of grief forever. It took years, but eventually, with the support of her family and friends, the pain of their daughter's loss dulled. They could finally remember and treasure their little ray of sunshine without too much sadness.

Lucy finally returned to work in the school system and concentrated on re-energizing her family life. Together, Jim and Lucy focused on their son, Willy, and planned a future where Willy could be anything he wanted to be. As Willy's enthusiasm for searching for minerals consumed his every weekend, he began to research how to make a career of it. Willy was hooked when he came across a program at the University of British Columbia that offered a degree in Mineral Exploration and Technology. Stars danced in his eyes whenever he talked about his future in a mineral-rich province like BC.

Jim and Lucy slowly came to accept their dreams were not his dreams. After months of discussions with anyone who could advise them, they set up new wills, ensuring their homestead would always be available to their descendants. As Jim well knew, land like theirs would be hard to replace. If Willy or his future children returned to Bella Coola, the land would be there for them to use. In the interim, the land could be leased out and maintained for Willy or their grandchildren should they come home.

"Mom!" Lucy turned to see her son jogging towards her. "Did you pick up the mail?"

"Yes, *mon cher*, I did."

"So? Did I get a letter from the university? It should be here by now. They said letters would be going to successful applicants by May 30."

Seeing the anxiety on her son's face made her relent, so she put him at ease. "Yes, it was. I thought maybe you'd like to wait and open it when your father gets home. What do you think?"

"I don't think I can wait that long. Dad won't be home until six or later. Let me see it-please?"

Lucy never could resist her son's pleadings. She opened her purse and took out the long envelope with the distinctive logo of the University of British Columbia on it. She waved it towards her son, then pulled it back to her chest. "You can have it if you promise not to open it. Another few hours aren't going to kill you. It would mean the world to your father if he was there to see the expression on your face."

"Alright, alright. Now hand it over. *Please.*" Willy was transferring his weight from one foot to the other, his eyes alight with excitement. When Lucy handed him the envelope, Willy held it gently, flipping it over, then holding it up to the sunlight in an attempt to see the contents. A concerned look crossed his face as doubts crept in.

"You needn't worry. Your grades were excellent in your senior year, and the results of your SAT exams were first-rate. I'm sure you'll leave us soon for the big city."

"Man, I hope so. You know what I mean. I'll miss you and this place, but I can hardly wait to go."

Lucy felt a knife stabbed through her chest at the thought of their only son moving away. She pushed it aside and replaced it with a positive attitude. Willy could sense her moods quickly, and the last thing she wanted was for him to feel guilty about leaving home.

"I know you are. We're excited for you. You'll come back for the summers, and then we'll go down and see you for Christmas just as we planned. It's going to be an adventure, that's for sure." Lucy grabbed his arm and leaned her head into Willy's shoulder as he chattered enthusiastically about the preparations they needed to make. Together, they walked to her car.

Tonight, the Taylor family would proudly celebrate another new beginning filled with hope. Jim would embrace his son's future, whatever it may hold. He had prepared their son well, just as his father had for him. The legacy they'd created would continue.

~

Thanks for reading *Finding Hope*.

Want to know how the next generation of the Taylor family endure the uncertainty caused by the chaos from climate change? ***All for Love***, book 1 in my *Safe Haven* series, will keep you guessing as the family tries to find their safe haven in a changing world.

Keep reading to find out more or to leave a review for *Finding Hope*.

DEAR READER

I hope you enjoyed *Finding Hope* and its glimpse of life in the 1930s and 40s in Canada. After listening to the stories of my family and researching the issues of the times, I gained a deeper empathy for their struggles and the reason they became the people they were and, therefore, their influence on me. Please post a review online if you enjoyed this story. Reviews are incredibly helpful to an author's success. They help readers find the books they love and motivate authors to keep writing those books.

You can review wherever you purchased *Finding Hope* and Goodreads and BookBub.

I always gain a new perspective when hearing from readers who identify with my books. I'm working on my next story, so visit my website www.LynnBoire.com, sign up for my newsletter or email me at Lynn@LynnBoire.com to stay in touch and learn about my new releases.

Cheers,
Lynn Boire

ACKNOWLEDGMENTS

Although *Finding Hope* is a work of fiction, the main events are inspired by the memoirs of my family and their close friends. They encouraged me to share some of their stories as Canadiana, so there would be an understanding of their struggles during the 'dirty thirties' and beyond. Any resemblance to actual people is unintentional and merely a result of imaginative compilation.

Heartfelt thanks go out to the Boire, Larose, Demers, and Beaulac families from the Debden and Big River area in central Saskatchewan for sharing their challenges. From their memoirs I learned that sometimes all we can pray for is the strength to move forward when everything seems against us, hoping and trusting that our moral compass will eventually bring us to a better place. I hope you have enjoyed this story.

As always, I genuinely appreciate the feedback and assistance from my ARC team. Hugs to Darlene Y, Anne E, Gina M, Dave, and Irene U, and my big sister, Angie.

To my husband Ron, my best friend Tricia, my precious children and grandson your heartfelt encouragement means the world to me.

I wouldn't have realized my lifelong dream to be an author without the generous support and guidance of the Vancouver Island Romance Authors chapter in Victoria, B.C., especially my mentor Jacqui Nelson. My appreciation goes out to Sarah Stewart and Alice Valdal who offered their valuable insights on my book. I know that my fellow writers' perceptive questions and remarks helped me make this a better novel. Thank you!

PRAISE FOR LYNN BOIRE

All for Love

"It's what many of us have feared....the time climate change becomes a reality. *All for Love* is about a family enduring all the trials, tribulations, and uncertainty they face, trying to find a new normal in the midst of chaos. Riveting!" ~ *Dave*

"*All for Love* opens a readers' eyes to how easily the idea of security can shift. Prepare yourself for a thought provoking tale." ~ *Suki Lang*

All for Family

"Enjoyed this one tremendously!" ~ *Darlene Y.*

"I really enjoyed the snappy dialogue. Perceptive glimpses into an Intention Living lifestyle opened my thoughts on this way of life." ~ *Karen G.*

All for Peace

"A refreshing novel that shows no one is perfect, but with love and honesty, relationships can work. Loved it." ~ *B Johnson*

"It was hard to put the novel down, the intriguing plot of romance, illusions, and murder kept me engaged until the end." ~ *A. Evans*

ABOUT THE AUTHOR

I write contemporary domestic suspense that reveals how families who avoid conflict find the confidence to voice their opinions and fulfill their dreams. In my stories, it's all about imperfect people finding unconditional love.

Following a lifelong dream to become a published author wasn't an easy decision. It wasn't until I joined the Vancouver Island Romance Authors group that I began to toss aside the self-doubts that had always assailed me. Their encouragement, recommendations, and support started my tenacious journey to learn the craft of writing. I'm constantly reading and studying material to grow as an author, and I've seldom been happier. I'm excited to be on the brink of a new career and hope you'll enjoy my novels.

I live in a seaside town on Vancouver Island in British Columbia, Canada. I use my deep appreciation of every part of my island home for the background in my stories. I feel a spiritual connection whenever I'm near a body of water. Nature puts everything in perspective, and all my doubts and worries float away. Even if a storm's strength frightens me, it also reminds me that—no matter what—all things pass. I'm blessed with many friends and family, including my husband, two grown children, a grandson, a step-daughter and her family.

LynnBoire.com

amazon.com/author/lynnboire
goodreads.com/author/show/20765007.Lynn_Boire
bookbub.com/authors/lynn-boire
facebook.com/lynnboire

Manufactured by Amazon.ca
Acheson, AB

12498223R00118